Matt is a disheartened, medically retired Royal Marine, who feels trapped back at home on South Uist, his self-esteem and drive abandoning him as he felt the Navy had. Travelling to Glasgow on family business, he intervenes to help a woman, Marieke and her small child, who he thinks are being mugged. He is unwittingly dragged into their nightmare, being hunted down by ruthless villains led by Nick Parson, a bent London copper, who will stop at nothing to silence Marieke and recapture the evidence she holds against him.

To keep them safe, Matt brings her to his home in Uist, thinking no one will find them in the peaceful hills of the remote community. But he underestimates Parson, who follows them like an unrelenting Hebridean Storm. They hide, but even here, nowhere is safe. Matt seeks help from friends and family, but will it be enough to escape with their lives and to protect the safety of those they love? And who is the enigmatic Murdo MacNeil? Can Matt rely on him to save their lives?

Acknowledgements

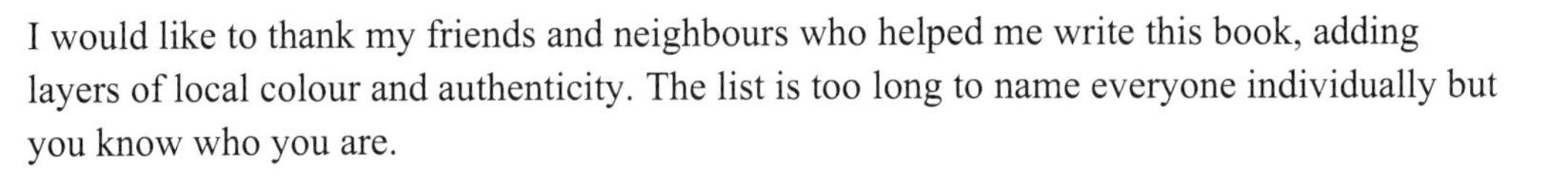

I would like to thank my friends and neighbours who helped me write this book, adding layers of local colour and authenticity. The list is too long to name everyone individually but you know who you are.

Thank you finally to my family who inspire me in all that I do.

Libby Patterson, South Uist, April 2016

Hebridean Storm

Published by Libby Patterson

ISBN 978-1-5220-118-42

This book is a work of fiction. Names, characters, places and incidents are the product of the author's imagination or are used fictitiously. Any resemblance to actual events, locales or persons, living or dead, is coincidental.

Chapter 1: Boxing Day 2013

It was a cold, icily crisp day. Matt sat on the edge of the rock, nearly two thousand feet up, not so much staring out at the Atlantic, but absorbing its vast wildness into his very soul. If you had been able to look through the eyes of the eagle circling the hill at that moment, you really would have wondered how he managed to balance so effortlessly on such a sheer edge. Yet as a child he had always been a bit of a mountain goat and revelled in the extreme challenges of nature. He felt alive, part of the wider universe as he stared out at the clear horizon. No matter how many times he saw or felt it, he marvelled at the sharpness of the sun on the water and the slow passage of the random white clouds.

But even for him, climbing Ben Mhor on Boxing Day morning, leaving a warm house and his family, to clamber through the grasping clumps of heather in the chilling wind was a bit extreme. He had needed to get out, to get away from his mother and sisters caring and fussing over him, to feel free and to prove that he was ok, to them and to himself, despite the views of the Navy Medical Board.

It had been two years, seven months and five days since Matt had last climbed. Up until last spring he had been fine, absolutely fine! As a junior officer in the Royal Marines, he had travelled the world, saved lives and negotiated some tricky situations. He had always wanted to join the services and was proud to be able to wear his Green Beret, believing that he was making a difference in the world. He had had a purpose to his life, until the world changed.

It had started with brain splitting headaches, then the fatigue, then the passing out. For a six foot, ginger marine to start fainting was the source of great amusement in the Mess and put down to overwork by the medics. But it didn't stop and soon became a liability. He raised his hand and absentmindedly scratched the six inch scar at the back of his shaved head. OK, he thought to himself, as he stretched his arm, if I hadn't had the Op, I wouldn't be able to do that.

Despite a couple of relapses and just not being able to rest, Matt finally made a full recovery.

They had given him a lump sum, offered training and glowing references, but they had taken his life away.

He would almost have felt better had he actually been injured in service. Then there would have been a reason for it, instead of some weird condition that nobody had ever heard of. He didn't like feeling sorry for himself. He felt guilty every time that he heard of troops being injured or killed. He just didn't know what he was going to do now and that really bugged him.

Matt shifted his weight on the rock. It wasn't that he felt insecure, it was just that the cold and damp from the mossy stone was beginning to seep through his jeans. He looked at his watch and took a sip from his water bottle. It was just past eleven. The clear air and exertion were definitely making him feel better, but time was passing and he needed to think about moving on. To go straight up and down seemed a bit boring and not much of a challenge. At this time of year though, he knew that he didn't have enough daylight to do the whole ridge. He could come back down behind the standing stone on the old water board track, but that would mean a trudge along the main road. There wouldn't be many cars about today to hitch a ride from. The single track tarmac road that ran close to the coast would be deserted and depressingly bleak after the splendour of the mountain. He didn't want to do that.

He picked himself up and stepped back to the track. It was rocky here, but he knew it would turn to heather and gorse underfoot as he got higher and he would hardly be able to see the path. It was because of this that he loved the wildness of the South Uist hills.

As he climbed higher the wind began to feel stronger and he felt that unmistakeable sense of dampness in the breeze. From nowhere a heavy dark cloud was beginning to close in around the mountain peak. It felt as if it was closing in around him too. He knew it could only be a matter of time before he would be drenched by a vicious, wind driven squall. The question was whether it would be a 10 minute downpour or would it last the rest of the day?

Right, he thought. A sprint to the top, or as far as I can get, then if the weather still looks grim I'll head back.

Matt enjoyed hill running, the "as far as I can get" was really only an afterthought, as he wanted to get to the top, to prove to himself that he was better. Setting his watch to time his run, he set off, focussed only on his goal of reaching the summit cairn.

He had been running for about ten minutes, his pace was steady, his breathing and rhythm good despite the uneven undergrowth. He had warmed up, even though it had started to rain. He was confident that he would get to the top before the weather forced him to turn back. He probably would have too, if it hadn't been for the out of place rustle of bracken and the hint of movement in the heather that just caught the corner of his eye.

He jogged on the spot and turned around to look across the harsh terrain. Had he been seeing things? It must have been an animal. How could there be somebody else up here? Part of him wanted to run on, convinced that he had made a mistake, but if there was someone up here they could be in trouble.

He cupped his hands to his mouth and called "hello". There was no response. This was daft. Why would somebody be lying in the heather on top of a mountain on Boxing Day and waving at passers-by?

"Hello" he called again. He paused ... nothing. He turned and started to run on again, annoyed at stopping. He had only run a few paces when he thought that he saw it again, to his left. Just by a small boulder sticking out of the moss, he was sure he could see the bushes rustling against the direction of the wind. What was it? It was about 200 yards away and he was fairly sure that it was not an animal, it would have been too big. After a second, it was the sound of human groaning floating faintly on the wind that sent him jogging in the direction of the moving bush.

It began to rain harder now, sharp spikes hitting the back of his head and shoulders. It was going to be a nasty one. He rubbed the palms of his hands against his temples as his head began to ache, annoyed at his escape being disrupted. He began to clamber across the hill towards the direction of the sound, still thinking that he was wasting time as the hidden boulders and rocks beneath the heather began to slow his progress down. He caught his left shin against a sharp rock, which caused him to hiss profanities at the inanimate object. He stopped and looked ahead, squinting his eyes, looked again. He cupped his hands to his mouth and yelled, "Hello, I'm coming!" For now, he was sure that he could see a human leg.

He moved faster as he now had a purpose, ignoring the scratches and scrapes along the way. In a few minutes, he found himself staring at the supine figure of a middle aged man, lying in what looked like a very unnatural position beside a rock. His thick grey short cropped hair was matted with blood and his left arm lay at a contorted angle.

Matt squatted down beside him, and fumbled under his collar for a pulse on his neck. Despite his greyish colour the man's heart beat strongly. Matt breathed a sigh of relief and began to assess his injuries. As he started to check for broken bones, the man groaned.

"You with us then mate?" Matt asked.

The man grunted in reply.

"Happy Christmas to you too," sighed Matt. Apart from what looked like a dislocated shoulder, the man didn't seem to have any broken bones. The gash on his head did appear to be more blood than actual wound, as usual with a head injury, so Matt hoped it wasn't as bad as it first looked.

The man seemed to be slowly gaining consciousness finally giving a sharp "Shit, that hurts!" when Matt brushed his left arm.

He opened his eyes and peered up. They were clear and strong; he was obviously in pain, but assessing his own situation. Matt was relieved that he wasn't going to have to deal with one of the island's more wayward characters.

"Sorry, can you help me sit up a bit," said the man in a low voice. "I seem to have got myself in a wee bit of bother." He spoke with what Matt always thought of as a posh Glasgow accent. It was a standing family joke that that there was no such thing as a posh Weegie, but he had known some senior officers who, although they had polished their vowels, had never been able to lose their roots. This was the hardness that Matt heard in the man's voice.

"Well that's one way of putting it, I guess. I'm Matt, who are you, and what're you doing up here?"

"Murdo, Murdo MacNeil, like you perhaps, trying to escape Christmas." He shifted his weight and Matt helped as the Glaswegian used his legs to push himself up slightly. He winced as he moved and shook his head slowly.

"Hey, don't take it so fast. Where does it hurt?"

"My legs seem OK, but there is something odd about my arm here." He paused, trying to hold his shoulder but flinched even at his own touch. Pausing to catch his breath he strained to remember. "I must have tripped and hit my head because it feels like I've used it as a battering ram. I feel sort of dizzy as if the whole world is just slightly at the wrong angle, but apart from that I'm fine." He laughed at his own joke, as if to lighten his own mood.

"That's OK then," agreed Matt. He fished his mobile phone out of one of his pockets and flipped it on. "Just as well really, as we are on our own, no signal up here." The rain had subsided to a miserable sort of drizzle. Matt rummaged in another pocket and pulled out a bottle of water and a packet of extra strong mints. He opened the water and handed Murdo the bottle.

"Just a little sip mind, don't want you throwing up." He unwrapped the sweets, took one himself and offered the pack. "A little sugar might help; sorry I haven't got anything stronger."

Murdo took a mint. He sat simply looking at the ground trying to refocus himself. Matt looked around, assessing the situation. "You warm enough?" he asked, resignedly shrugging himself out of his own jacket.

"Looks like the rain is going to stop. I suggest we keep you warm and still till it does, then we'll strap that arm and try and move closer to the road to get some signal."

Murdo nodded, mumbling his thanks, as Matt placed his jacket around the older man's shoulders, and hunkered down beside him. It wasn't too long before the rain stopped as the clouds passed and the sun re-emerged to warm their backs. Matt stretched his shoulders in appreciation. Murdo raised his head and turned to Matt.

"OK, we'd better get on with it then lad. As you don't have a wee dram to dull the pain, you'd just better get on and strap my arm, so we can move."

Matt used a combination of his belt and Murdo's scarf to strap the injured arm to the man's body, and slowly helped him to his feet. Murdo placed his good arm on Matt's shoulder and they slowly made their way down the mountain side. They stopped several times for Murdo to rest and for Matt to try his phone, but there was still no signal. They chatted about this and that on the way down, nothing of consequence, but Murdo seemed to thaw a little and despite his injuries was sure footed enough. Perhaps he is feeling better, thought Matt.

It was when they had got as far as the reservoir, which is only just above the road that Matt's phone did actually spring to life with a clear rendition of the "Scooby Doo" theme tune.

"That will be the phone then," quipped Murdo, who was, despite the walk and pain in his arm, beginning to feel a bit more human.

"Yes, and I bet I know who it will be," sighed Matt as they stopped. He did know who it was; his mother with a typically short text message:

'Where are you? We will be eating at four. Will you be back?'

He looked at his watch, it was four thirty. He suddenly felt very hungry and hoped that they had saved him some Boxing Day curry.

"Better report in," he commented to Murdo as he called home.

"Hello there, it's me."

There was a pause.

"-Well I didn't mean to be this long to be honest, but I found someone hurt on the hillside and have had to help him down."

Another pause

"I'm sure it doesn't just happen to me. Is there any chance of a lift? We are heading towards the Stoneybridge Road end. He's in no state to drive, we can either bring him home, or we may have to take him to the hospital." Matt did wonder where Murdo's car was, but as he wasn't about to drive, they would have to deal with it later. He continued,

"Oh, Ok then, that's great. Err, he's called Murdo."

Murdo was now standing upright, with a determined look in his eyes. "Thank you for your help, but I am not going to hospital. I'm sure I will be fine after a good night's sleep. I will just need a lift back to my hotel if that's ok and I'll sort my car out tomorrow."

Matt was a little taken aback by the Glaswegian's attitude. He didn't fancy spending the rest of the day in casualty either, but there was no need to be like that. That hardness was back in Murdo's voice.

"One of my sisters is coming to get us. Kate will be glued to her laptop working at something, so it will probably be Iona, she's pregnant and ended up the duty driver this Christmas. Mum says to bring you back for some dinner. My aunt Liz is there, she's the duty nurse on St Kilda. She knows how to deal with the walking wounded, so can give you the once over. I wouldn't argue with those two, but it is up to you."

"Thank you, I just don't want to put anyone out."

"Well you have little option right now." Matt gave a chuckle.

They made their way down closer to the road, and headed north for a few minutes. They came to a passing place, by a small wall and a gate leading into a field.

"We'll stop here and wait for her, she can turn the car in MacDonald's gateway over there. I will let them know exactly where we are."

While Matt texted, Murdo looked around him. These people amazed him, they were, to him, in the middle of nowhere, yet this lad still knew whose field he was standing in front of. It wasn't that he was ungrateful and to be truthful the thought of a hot meal was very welcome. He just didn't know if he was up to fending off all the questions that would be asked about his being there.

They were standing in an uncomfortable silence when Iona pulled up. She turned the car around. Matt opened the door and climbed into the back of her little red Nissan, leaving Murdo to fold himself into the front seat.

"Hello, I'm Iona, are you sure you are comfortable?" she beamed at Murdo with compassion and friendliness. Then, without waiting for a response, looking in the rear view mirror, she glared at Matt. "Mum has been worried sick about you; you could at least have left a note or something to say where you were going. If she hadn't heard from you, she was going to call the Coast Guard, it was only Aunty Liz coming round that calmed her down. The two of them are on the G&Ts already so we had better eat soon!"

"And that's my fault?"

"Well, I had to deal with it. Kate's been stuck on the phone and Iain's had to go back already!"

Murdo tried to suppress a smile. Maybe this wouldn't be so bad after all. He liked this feisty young lady, and also hoped there would be a G&T on offer for him.

Matt groaned inwardly. Her husband had returned to work, that's why his sister was so ratty. Iona was the younger of his twin sisters; she had always been the most serious of the three of them. Although the youngest of the family, when their father had left, it was she who had pulled them all together. She could be frighteningly direct. Matt felt sorry for her husband sometimes. She had been having problems with her blood pressure during her pregnancy and had to give up her job as a Social Worker early. Christmas was important to her, and she was not in the most sympathetic frame of mind to her brother's disappearing act as she saw it.

They turned left off the main road onto a windy single track lane, signposted as the village of Bornish. There didn't seem to be much of a village to Murdo, just a dozen houses spread out around a loch which the road seemed to meander past. More water than land he thought. It had already started to get dark and the outside lights switched on as they rolled up the drive to a whitewashed, square building. Originally it was a bungalow, but was modernised some years ago to allow the family to extend into the roof space. It was functional rather than a pretty house, yet the scent of the peat fire made it very welcoming.

Iona manoeuvred herself out of the car and walked round to open the door for Murdo. "Careful, there are icy patches," she warned as she led him to a side door; she didn't wait for Matt.

The door led straight into a rectangular kitchen, with a big green Aga stove and a well-used kitchen table at which two women sat. Matt followed in behind his sister and their guest.

"Mum, this is Murdo McNeil, Murdo this is my mum, Seonag Macaulay, and my aunt Liz MacDonald. Despite how he looks Murdo says he is definitely not going to hospital."

The introductions over, the two women exchanged glances. Liz raised an eyebrow as Seonag got up to welcome him in. She started to ask what had happened and if there was anyone they should contact and pulled up a chair for him.

Liz stood and said, "Why don't I take him out into the back room and see what the extent of the damage is, and then we will know what to do next. Iona, call your sister to help me, she shouldn't be working on Boxing Day anyway." She turned to Murdo and smiled, "Don't worry I'm not propositioning you or going to bite, I'm a nurse, why don't you follow me. We'll maybe need to find you dry clothes too, eh?"

They all left the room, leaving Seonag and Matt standing together.

"I'm sorry; I didn't mean to worry you. You should be used to me by now. I just wanted to...well you know... Do something!"

Despite the fact that he was wet and muddy Seonag wrapped her arms around her son and they stood quietly and hugged each other.

"Yes, I know," she whispered. "But you have plenty of time to do things, stop beating yourself up trying to do everything now." As she let go she told him, "You should go and have a shower then come back and help me set the table. Who is he anyway?"

Matt briefly explained what had happened and the little he knew.

"Don't worry," laughed Seonag, "Liz will get the details out of him. You know what she's like."

Matt stood under the shower enjoying the hot water beating off his body. He heard a loud groan and expletives coming from the back room. He smiled, guessing that it was Liz "fixing" Murdo's shoulder. She would be telling him to "man up".

When he re-entered the kitchen all four women were sat around the table, their heads together. Liz was talking in a low excited whisper, while his mother was just shaking her head, laughing as were the two girls.

"What've you done with him?" he asked.

"He's just having a wee rest, I've given him your old tracksuit to wear, is that ok? I put his clothes on the rail in the bathroom."

"Did he not tell you about his family and why he's here?" asked his mother.

"No, what?" Matt pulled up a chair.

"Well," smiled Liz, bustling with excitement and her amusement at Murdo's story. "He says that he works for the Poileas, not a copper, some sort of office job. He's been working away in London, but is now back in Glasgow."

"Tell him the good bit," urged Seonag.

"The reason he had to leave Glasgow? Well he says that he has been married three times. All his ex-wives and nine children and three grandchildren live in and around Glasgow and Edinburgh. They were arguing about who he'd spend Christmas with now that he's back, so he decided to spend it in the wilds out here to avoid the grief."

"You didn't get their names and ages, Aunty Liz, you're slipping!" laughed Kate.

"We can't all be young journalist of the year," her aunt retorted.

"Do you believe that?" Liz asked Matt, shaking her head in disbelief. But he didn't get a chance to answer, as they heard a noise on the stairs. Their guest was about to join them.

When Murdo rejoined the family they were scattered around preparing for a meal. He could tell by their sideways glances that they had been talking about him. He wondered if they believed a word of the story he had told them.

"Come and sit down." Liz pointed to a chair at the table, "You didn't change your clothes?"

"No, I'm not a track suit sort of person, I'm fine. It's very good of you to help me and feed me like this. I have to admit I'm ready for my dinner now and this smells better than the food at the hotel."

They all laughed, they didn't mention that the chef at the hotel was one of their cousins and a good friend. Everyone tucked into their curry hungrily as it was later than planned. There was silence as they ate, each one lost in their own thoughts.

Murdo took the opportunity to assess the company. Matt looked ex-military he thought. The two older women must be near their fifties and they were, to his eye, stylishly dressed, not what he thought of as the typical Hebridean Crofter.

But what was that? He thought. The media stereotypes were all based on 1950s images. These were obviously modern women. Where did they buy their clothes, he wondered, he hadn't seen any shops? The internet? Amazon must make a fortune here.

There was something about the younger girls, the pregnant Iona and her sister Kate whom he hadn't spoken to yet. Kate had short cropped hair, just long enough to have a hint of a curl. Combined with her strong intelligent features she was strikingly attractive, but obviously not to be messed with. The girls shared the same eyes, cheekbones and infectious smiles. Iona, with her long dark hair and those big brown eyes, looked amazing too. Her pregnancy gave her an extra glow. They were so different but yet...

"You are twins?" he hadn't meant to say it out loud, but they didn't seem to mind.

"Yes," smiled Kate.

"Sorry, it's not immediately obvious, but there is something I couldn't put my finger on."

"We're what are called mirror image twins. We are the exact opposite of each other. Iona is the nice, caring person who helps people, while I have no mercy in exposing those who have done wrong and bringing them down to where they should be." She laughed, thumping the table jokingly with her fist for emphasis.

"It's not quite good twin; evil twin," joined in Iona. "We both do it for the greater good, or something like that, as mum would say!" She was mimicking her mother and laughing.

"I brought them all up to be honest and now I have to live with the consequences." Her mother agreed, joining in with the joke.

Murdo turned to Matt wanting to bring him into the conversation. "Is that why you became a squaddie? Because it was the honest thing to do?"

"I am not a "squaddie," he answered flatly, as he continued with his meal.

"He was a Marine," explained his mother, "medically retired, it's inter-service rivalry, he doesn't like being called a squaddie."

Here we go again, Matt thought, "Just to be clear, I wasn't injured, just some freak condition. Thanks for dinner mum, I have a couple of things to do, so do excuse me. Glad you are feeling better Murdo."

"Hang on, I didn't mean to offend you." Murdo started, "It's just that, well you practically saved my life today... I'd like to know a bit more about you, so I can at least tell people who it was who saved me."

"Some other time maybe." Matt had finished his meal. He noisily pushed his chair back as he got up from the table. It wasn't that he had that much to do or that he was being intentionally rude, it was just that he knew he would not be able to stop his mother and aunt describing his illness and operation in full technicolour detail. He didn't think that he could sit through it again. She would be telling the truth but it would have such a positive spin, he didn't want to hear how lucky he was, or hear Liz's gory medical descriptions.

Seonag watched her son leave the room. He heard her start explaining as he walked away.

"He had always wanted to join the services and was so proud to be able to wear his Green Beret. He really was making a difference." She explained his passion not as a need to be in a war zone but by the fact that while some people could watch the terrible things on the TV news and say, "how awful"; Matt felt that he had the ability and duty to do something about them. He knew that he did in his own small way. He had a purpose to his life, until his world changed.

"After what seemed an age of prodding, poking, tests scans and x-rays, he was diagnosed with a rare neurological condition, a Chiari malformation. The good news was that it wasn't fatal; the bad news that if he didn't have neurosurgery immediately he could lose the use of his arms and legs within two years."

"He had the operation and despite a couple of relapses and just not being able to rest, finally made a full recovery. To this day, we still argue as to whether going off-road mountain biking two weeks after surgery could have anything to do with him being rushed back into hospital. But he endured it all in good heart with humour and spirit." She sighed. "It was what happened afterwards that has broken his heart. The Navy were very good to him while he was ill, but the Medical board took months reviewing his case and finally decided that even though he had returned to full fitness, due to the nature of his condition and operation he was no longer fit for military service. He even wrote to his commanding officer and offered to work in the store or sweep the floors, but the answer was final, not even a desk job. Last November he was finally discharged from the Military. Yes, they gave him a lump sum, offered training, and glowing references but he just doesn't know what to do with himself. Instead of being happy to be alive, he's angry with the world and with himself."

"Has he considered the Police Force or emergency services? I could perhaps give him a couple of contacts. I certainly owe him a favour after today. The new Police Scotland Force is recruiting now."

"Phfff," interrupted Kate, "I think he needs something worthwhile, not to join that white elephant. Poorly paid folk in call centres that have no idea where they are sending the local Poileas."

A penny dropped for Murdo. He knew there was something he had recognised about the girl, Kate Macaulay. She was a journalist and had recently been writing scathing attacks on the Police re-organisation, the hidden costs of saving money and the inefficient bureaucracy as she saw it. She probably had a point, he thought, but that was never to be said out loud in the circles he moved in. He made a mental note to look up Matt's records.

"All the same, I like to pay my debts." He took a couple of business cards out of his wallet. Could you give him these, if he ever wants to get in touch, next time he's in town maybe?"

As Seonag took the cards from him a car horn sounded loudly outside. Liz sighed. pushing her chair back she got to her feet. "I am afraid that will be JJ come to pick me up. He's not planning to come in; he's dropping me off then heading on to check the sheep. It's hard on them in this weather. D' you want a lift to your hotel or car Murdo, we're heading north?"

Happy to escape further questions, Murdo felt that it was a good moment to extract himself. Nodding his thanks, he explained how an early night would probably be what he needed after his ordeal.

Murdo put on his still damp jacket as hugs and thanks were exchanged between the sisters and nieces. Matt did not reappear. Kate was sent to tell him that Murdo was leaving. She found him sound asleep, still half dressed and decided not to disturb him.

Thanking everyone profusely Murdo followed Liz out to the car. Disappearing into the night, Murdo left as quickly and mysteriously as he had arrived. As her daughters cleared away the dinner dishes, Seonag looked at his business cards.

"Odd," she murmured, fiddling with them between her thumb and forefinger. There was his name, a couple of phone numbers and an email address, but no job title or company or department name. "How strange."

~~~
~~~

Chapter 2: April 2014

Spring came slowly in South Uist. It wasn't until the end of January that there seemed to be any semblance of real daylight. February and March brought wild gales that made even the most weather-beaten old crofter pause for breath. By April the talk was all of lambs and calves. The spring flowers were starting to appear on the machair and the constant wind had lost its bite. Mainland Scotland was pre-occupied with the devolution debate, but in the Macaulay household the family was more interested in Iona's pregnancy, the forthcoming baby and more immediately, the health of mother and child.

Kate was coming home for the holidays to visit her sister. She had been living in Fort William, house sitting for friends who were abroad for two years, using it as her base to follow the various devolution debates and campaigns. The relationship between England and Scotland was at an all-time low. Misinformation from the Westminster camp had sparked over-exaggerated claims by some of the Nationalists, leading to ill-tempered exchanges, negative campaigning, and even violence in some quarters. Kate was leading her own campaign to get to the facts and to unmask those who she thought were trying to defraud the Scottish people for their own ends. This had kept her very busy, but had made her enemies on both sides. She felt it was sensible to keep a low profile for the time being.

Iona was staying at her mum's. She'd slept in. She woke up feeling groggy. Her ankles seemed to swell the moment she put them on the floor. She felt as if she had the hangover from hell, without having had a drink. She rubbed her bump.

"I do hope you're feeling better than me, pumpkin," she sighed.

"You've got to stop calling that child Pumpkin, it'll grow up with a complex!" It was Matt in the doorway with a cup of tea. "Mum's gone to the airport to get Kate. I have to encourage you to stay in bed."

"But I have things to do. I am not ill, just pregnant. Iain will be home next week and I have my own house to sort out."

"Well that's a matter of opinion, isn't it?" His sister shot him a sideways look. "About how well you are, not Iain coming back. Anyway, let him do the sorting when he gets back."

"No, it's not fair, he's been working offshore."

"Huh, he's probably spent the last few months playing cards and computer games. They won't have been doing much building on the rigs during the storms."

Iona shrugged. She didn't really have the energy to argue with her brother, but that had never stopped her before. She very much missed her husband and was defensive about him. She was sure she would feel better when he got home.

"At least he has a job," she retorted, but regretted the words as soon as she had spoken them. She saw her brother's shoulders drop and his expression change as he put down her tea.

"Och I'm sorry Matt, I'm just crabby, hormones, I didn't mean..."

"Yeah, I think I got hormones too, drink your tea. I've lit the fire, and I'm going to help Callum with his lambs. I'll be back at lunch time."

Iona sat back on the bed and drank her tea. She thought Matt had been a bit better of late, but it was still too easy to burst his bubble. He hadn't used to be like that. It's a shame, she thought. I would quite like my brother back as well as my husband. The baby kicked.

"I know, you want them too, don't you Pumpkin." She said out loud, rubbing her tummy.

She looked over to the window. She heard the gentle rumble of a distant car engine.

"Is that Matt leaving or Kate arriving?" It got louder. "Yeah, Come on Pumpkin, Auntie Kate is here!" She pulled on some clothes, tidied her hair back and made her way down stairs. She wanted to be in the kitchen before they arrived, she didn't want them to see how much it hurt her to move.

She was sitting in the armchair by the stove, sipping her tea, when Kate and her mother came in. Hugs and kisses were exchanged, tea made and gossip caught up on. When Seonag nipped out to bring some shopping in from the car, Kate turned to her sister;

"You look like shit!"

"I look like you!"

"Don't be funny, you are not fooling me or mum, what's wrong?"

"I dunno, I just feel rubbish and sore. We have so much to do before this one arrives but I just don't have the energy and that is stressing me out."

"What do you mean sore?" asked her mother now standing in the doorway.

"Och, it's just my back, when I walk, sit and lie down and I pee constantly and don't sleep, that's all. I don't have the energy to do anything. I'm meant to be going to Glasgow this week to pick up the new car, I was going to ask you to come with me," she nodded to her sister, "but I just can't do it."

"Never mind all that, I think you should see someone, have you called the doctor or the midwife?" Her mum sounded determined.

"You know what they're like, they will either tell me to rest...but I've too much to do...or try and send me to Glasgow, and I am not going anywhere without Iain." She folded her arms across her chest. Both Seonag and Kate knew that tone, Iona's stubbornness was legendary. But it was also a fact of life on the islands that as good as the medical services and the Uist and Barra Hospital was, they knew their limitations. People with medical emergencies and complications in conditions such as pregnancy often found themselves being sent to Lewis or the mainland for treatment and this is what Iona wanted to try and avoid.

"OK, OK, let's take one thing at a time. If you rest, we'll sort out things for you. If the car is so important, Kate or Matt can collect it for you, can't you?"

Kate didn't reply, but furrowed her brow and shifted slightly in her seat.

"It is important as the baby seat won't work in our two door Nissan. We've arranged to trade it in, and got a good deal, but it must be done by the end of next week or we lose the discount. I told Iain I'd go."

"If that's what's worrying you, we'll sort it one way or another but mum is right, you need to take it easy in the meantime. Why don't you go through and put your feet up on the sofa, we'll spend the afternoon watching a girly film and drinking hot chocolate, like we used to. How does that sound?"

Iona gave a weak smile and nodded. Tears had formed in the corners of her eyes; she hated feeling so weak and vulnerable. Seonag walked over and took her daughter in her arms and gently stroked her hair.

"Go on, your sister's right, I'll get you a blanket."

Matt came home shortly after the girls had decamped to the living room to watch the film. Seonag explained what had transpired, she also told him that she felt it would be difficult for Kate to go, as she had based herself in Fort William and was in the middle of researching an article.

Matt could never really keep up with Kate's various stories. He knew that she was staying in a friend's house to give her some degree of anonymity, but thought that was a bit extreme for a journalist in Scotland. He spoke with his sisters and agreed to take the little Nissan to Glasgow the following Monday. It clashed with a trip to watch his friend Callum's debut football game for the “Saints” the local team, playing in Inverness. It was to be a crucial match as they had just been promoted from the Uist and Barra League to the Highlands and Islands Amateur league. It was going to be a big day. But he understood how helping Iona to unwind was important right now. He booked his ferry crossing. He could travel to the mainland from either end of the island. The choice was between a short crossing via Skye with a six hour drive through the highlands to Glasgow or a five hour ferry crossing from Lochboisdale to Oban with only a short drive into the city. It was another aspect of island life everyone was just used to. On a pleasant day, the Oban boat gave you the opportunity to relax watching the dolphins and whales that followed the ferry. In winter, it was simply to be endured. Matt didn’t mind either way, he was sure to find someone on either boat to talk to. The choice was really down to the timetable and when he would get into Glasgow. Iona was keen to minimise the driving time, both for her brother and for her car, so the decision was made. It was Matt’s choice to book a room in a hotel on Argyll Street, close to the Uist Triangle in Glasgow. It was a part of town well known to the islanders on their trips to the mainland. I may as well have a good night out while I am there, he thought.

He set off early on the Monday morning, at least it was only a ten minute drive to Lochboisdale. He was packed off with the garage details and his mother’s inevitable shopping list. Seonag also gave him one of Murdo MacNeil’s business cards.

“You might want to look him up,” she laughed as she slipped it into his pocket. Matt doubted it.

The ferry crossing was thankfully smooth. Matt enjoyed his full cooked breakfast and kept topped up on numerous cups of tea. He talked to a couple of people; an old teacher from school and a couple friends of his mother’s. He read the newspaper and listened with interest to the different conversations on the forthcoming referendum. Kate was right, passions were running high, with the most unexpected people holding strong views. In the bar, there was a group of lassies, who looked like a hen party, arguing about the pros and cons of using the pound. He laughed as one who looked more unsteady than she should do at that time of day declared she wanted a Scottish currency and would call it “the thistle”, which prompted more vigorous debate. He went on deck as they approached the inner isles. The Island of Mull and the headland of Ardnamurchan looked so close and clear that you could almost step onto them. The sharp features and profile of the hills and rock contrasted between the sky and the sea. He could see people in Tobermory going about their business, tiny in the panoramic vastness.

Oban was bustling with the start of the season. The mainland always felt different. The noises, the rush, the busloads of tourists thronging around the quayside. The scenery had lost its wildness. Mankind was now in control rather than the elements. Or at least that is what they thought. It was slow progress through the holiday traffic along the seafront out of town. He drummed his fingers on the steering wheel hoping that at least some of the cars and mobile homes were not heading to Glasgow. The frustration wasn't that he wanted to be in the city. He enjoyed driving and wanted to take advantage of the open road. After the narrow single track roads of Uist it was good to get some speed up and hear the throb of the engine. He passed the "Green Welly" cafe and shop at Tyndrum and found himself singing along loudly with Runrig as he drove around Loch Lomond. The narrow twists and turns of the famous road on the edge of the loch made for an exhilarating drive, but soon opened up into a dual carriageway as Matt finally turned left at Tarbert towards Glasgow. The roads got wider and the traffic built up, converging from left and right into a nose to tail queue towards the city. It was a different world from the one he had woken up in that morning. Concrete and glass replaced the Machair and beaches, but he was happy, he needed the change. Perhaps he would enjoy a couple of days away. I should at least try, he told himself.

Things didn't go quite so smoothly at the garage. The car wasn't ready and he was going to have to call back the next day. He would have to rearrange his return crossing, but it wasn't the end of the world, Calmac who provided the lifeline ferry service to the islands were usually OK about such things. Returning to the hotel he had a quick meal then set out for a night out in the big city.

~~~

Chapter 3: Monday evening

The Park Bar is an old fashioned Scottish pub, situated in what is locally referred to as the Uist Triangle in Glasgow. On the corner with Grey Street, it was rather more than walking distance from Matt's Argyll Street Hotel, but worth the effort. Matt couldn't remember ever having had a dull night there or seeing any serious trouble. He was looking forward to a second dinner of one of their famous steak pies and enjoying whatever would be on. Despite the fact that there wasn't usually entertainment planned for a Monday night, there was a fiddle player and a girl on a tin whistle giving an impromptu performance in the corner of the bar. They provided a relaxing backdrop as Matt sat and chatted with the barmaid and a lad from Barra who had flown in for a job interview. They were helping the barmaid to compile questions for the next month's Gaelic quiz evening. Matt was planning to bring Kate over, and then appear really clever when he knew all the answers. He wasn't sure how much assistance they were really giving, but the craic was good. The talk turned to football and the "Saints" success. The timings being different to the national league, the start of the new football season was eagerly anticipated as a major social event for the young, (and not so
~~~

young), in the islands and the rivalry was just as fierce.

The Park Bar was owned by a family from Lochboisdale, and was often frequented by Uist folk when they were in town. It wasn't that he knew practically everyone in the bar as he would at home, but there was the familiar lilt to the conversation in either Gaelic or English. Local jokes and references were understood. He didn't feel like a foreigner in his own country when some Weegie thought that Uist was somewhere close to Largs.

The street outside was quiet at about eleven thirty when he decided to head back to his hotel. He stepped outside into the spring night; he could smell the traffic and the city; diesel and stale takeaways, very different from Uist. He looked around at the tenement flats, they had a rundown air to them, and he knew he would never feel comfortable with living that close together. He shivered and pulled his jacket on, looking over at the Chinese take away opposite. Despite the fact that he had eaten he bemoaned the fact that it was closed and he wouldn't be able to buy a final packet of chips to eat on the way home. Looking past the restaurant, over the cobblestoned road, he saw a woman in the alley. She was young, slight and dressed in skimpy denim shorts, with a half sleeved denim shirt as a jacket over a vest top. Her arms and legs were bare and looked cold. She tottered on strappy sandals that did not look man enough for the city streets. Hookers here, thought Matt, well that's a first, wait till I tell... His thoughts were interrupted as he realised that the woman had a small child who looked about eighteen months old with her. There was something disturbing about the scene. She had clumsily tried to lift the child, who was now struggling in her arms. It all just seemed a bit out of place, she was looking around her and trying to hurry, stumbling on the uneven surface juggling between the child and what looked like a large bag. He thought about offering to help her, but she had a desperate anxious look about her and he thought that he might frighten her. His intentions could be misinterpreted if she started screaming. She was heading away from the brightly lit bar disappearing into the gloom of the shadowy lane opposite, re- balancing her load against the tumble down wall and soothing the child before she continued on.

He was about to turn away when Matt became aware of some other figures in the alley. It wasn't that he could see them as such, more sense their presence. He wondered if they were customers of hers or drunks; but they weren't. He could only see their shapes at first, but their body language was obviously determined. They were heading towards her and not in a friendly way. She knew that too, because the moment she caught sight of them she turned quickly and started running back towards Matt. The child was screaming now and the girl was tripping over her bag. As she came closer to the road, towards the light she saw Matt. He could see her eyes wide and pleading. A look of sheer terror was etched upon her face. He'd seen that look before in war zones, but not in the centre of Glasgow. She made a split second decision. She kissed the child quickly on the forehead then almost threw him out of her arms toward the main road. He looked bewildered at his mother, "Run, copilul a alerga! Du-te, du-te, te iubesc!" She shrieked repeatedly. Matt didn't know what it meant, but got the gist as the little figure came crawling and stumbling onto the cobbled street towards him.

The street light on the corner threw a pool of dim light behind them, against it Matt saw that the two men were now running. One, a small wiry man, caught up with the girl, but ran past her; he was heading for the child. She was screaming even louder, Matt couldn't quite understand what was going on, but he didn't have time to think. He was closest. In one swift movement, he picked up the child and thrust him on top of a large council rubbish bin by the Chinese Take Away. It was wide, with a closed lid that dipped in the centre. "Sit" he ordered him, in a tone that he knew worked for dogs and "Nods" in the Marines. He just hoped it would work for a child. He turned to face the small wiry figure, ready to demand an explanation as the man stood breathless in front of him. He was holding his sides, breathing heavily and leaning forward slightly. "Look mate, I know this looks odd, but it's not your business so just walk away eh? There's a boyo."

To Matt this was getting stranger and stranger. Behind the Welshman, Matt could see that a stockier figure had caught up with the girl and was grappling with her, struggling to and fro in the light of the streetlamp. She was putting up a determined fight for one so slight. He thought that she almost had the better of him when, as their shadows loomed against the wall, Matt could see the man's raised arm and in his hand the silhouette of a syringe. He did not have time for conversation, but he did have the element of surprise. Not only was Taff not expecting to be hit, he was not expecting to be hit by a martial arts champion who was trained in unarmed combat. It had been a while, but his flying side kick launched Matt's right heel at the spot where the man's nose met his cheek bone. There was a satisfying crack as his nose broke, splintering cartilage, causing blood and gore to explode from his nostrils as he collapsed to the floor, yelping in shock and pain.

Matt didn't wait around, he charged roaring into the alley and threw himself bodily at the other man. While his kick had been a precision strike, this was an old fashioned rugby tackle, using his body weight to throw the attacker off his feet. They both rolled to the ground yet despite being winded, the man got up and grappled for Matt's jacket and hair. He had lost hold of the syringe in the process, but he wasn't giving up. He came at Matt with a vicious ferocity, shouting and swearing at his partner to help him. He was trying desperately to restrain Matt, clinging onto him with grim determination. Matt had no choice; he thrust his forearm under the man's chin and his other arm into his chest to shove him away. The assailant toppled backwards, and off balance as he hit the ground again, this time with force, his head hitting the uneven kerb with a sickening thud. For a split second there was silence, even the girl had stopped screaming. Had he killed him? Finally the man groaned, Matt breathed again knowing that he was alive, but he would have one hell of a headache in the morning.

Matt allowed himself to slide to the ground against the cold wall, he was shaking, his breathing rapid, and he could feel his head get hotter as the pounding behind his ears increased. He should call the police. He couldn't believe what had just happened, he didn't get into fights; this was the West end of Glasgow, not Helmand. He wondered if there was much difference.

To his left, the bulky male figure was curled in a foetal position moaning to himself. To his right the girl was half collapsed against the wall too. The syringe hanging off her jacket fell to the ground. It didn't seem to have lost much of its content.

"How're you doing?" he asked as he fumbled for his phone. She opened her eyes, staring in a disquieting way.

"Kazik? Kazik!" She shouted, her voice rising with anxiety.

"Oh shit, the kid!" Matt mumbled as he pulled himself to his feet. "Hang on, I'll get him." He stumbled over to the bin where the child was staring wide eyed like his mother. As he approached the boy, the figure on the floor was on all fours, holding his bloody face, but trying to get up. He looked up and cursed.

"You've broken my fucking nose, you'll... "

"Shut up and stay there or I'll break something else," snapped Matt. He kicked him over again just to make the point then stepped past him to the infant.

The child was dirty, sticky and definitely smelly, and Matt really didn't want to get too close to him. But strangely, he had stopped crying and was holding out his arms. Matt tentatively picked him up. Surprisingly, the youngster just relaxed in his arms and rested his head on his shoulder. As he returned to the alley with the child he started to dial 999, but stopped as he heard the sound of sirens and could see squad cars coming up Grey Street. He crouched down giving the boy to his mother.

"Don't worry," he smiled, "Help is on its way." She smiled weakly, but was shivering now and looked small and vulnerable. He took his jacket off and wrapped it round her shoulders. She clutched both her child and the bag, closed her eyes and said in barely audible faltering English.

"Please... help us."

~~~
~~~

Chapter 4: Late Monday Night: The Police Station

PC Jim Grey was a tubby little fellow who would never have got into the police force if the old fashioned height restrictions had still been in place, and many of his friends and family wondered how he got through the annual medicals and fitness tests. He was slightly older than Matt and had a pragmatic approach to policing. He called an ambulance for the two injured men and listened to the explanation about the girl being attacked, which she appeared to support with frantic little nods and pursed lips. The landlady from the Park Bar who had called 999 also vouched for Matt as a normally peaceable young man. She told Jim that she thought he was maybe ex-services. Jim explained that they would have to accompany him to the Police Station to make a statement but it was all a matter of procedure really. He didn't know what the Sergeant would think. "Have-a-go heroes", didn't normally wreak such destruction. In all the excitement, the syringe was not mentioned and had got lost somewhere in the alley.

The girl gave her name as Marieke Manover. She said, in very stilted English that she was newly arrived in Glasgow, and was looking for a hotel when attacked. She did not know who the men were. Any other questions that Jim asked, she simply shook her head, gesturing that she didn't understand. Matt didn't really believe her, he thought the men didn't look like muggers, they were too smartly dressed. But then what did muggers look like? He was also fairly sure that she had been targeted; she started running the moment she saw them and they went for the child after all.

It was a short drive to the Police Station, but the red tape and procedure seemed to take a lifetime to complete. This was despite the fact that Jim was fairly sure that he wasn't going to arrest anyone. They were in the local Police Sub-Station, which was staffed by himself, another PC, a sergeant who was in charge, along with a couple of admin staff. It had a secure room, an operations room and a suite of three interview rooms. It was not open to the public or able to hold prisoners for any length of time. As part of the new Police Scotland reorganisation, all that was only done at central stations now. It meant more ferrying of yobs about the city but tonight, as this was a minor incident, he thought he could deal with it quickly. When they had arrived there, the sergeant and his colleague had gone to another call. He settled the victims in a bleak waiting area and arranged tea. He knew what the boss would say about a child on the premises, so while their drinks came he rang the Police support services and explained the situation.

"Is the child in danger now?" asked a bored voice on the other end.

"No, a bit neglected, but not in danger. He is with his mother."

"Are you charging the mother with anything?"

"No, she's the victim."

"Well you don't need us then."

"But isn't one of you meant to attend if there's a child here?"

"Look, there are only four of us...one is off sick; one is on a training course and one is being investigated...that leaves me. If the wain's happy with his mam, and there are no charges being brought against her or her friend I have higher priorities. Call me if the situation changes."

The line went dead. Jim just looked at the receiver and slowly shook his head as he replaced it. But she had made a good point though. He popped his head around the door of an adjoining office.

"Can you do me a favour Sarah?" He asked a woman, working at a computer in the Operations room. "Can you do a search for me on Marieke Manover, and Matthew Macaulay? Do they have a record and see if there are any outstanding warrants for them," he paused, "UK and international ones?" He scratched his head, better to be sure. He didn't really believe that she was just looking for a hotel either. "I'm going to start interviewing Mr Macaulay, will you keep an eye on the girl and the kid? Bring the results through when you get them, oh, and if there is any ID or update from the two that went to the General that would be good too?" He gave a big grin. "Thanks."

In the waiting room, it was clear that the two didn't really know each other. They were seated at opposite ends of the room on the hard benches and didn't look as if they had been talking. Matt held his head in his hands, leaning forward, his elbows on his knees. She had her eyes closed, but was holding onto her child and that bag for dear life. Troubled girl, he thought, I may have to get an interpreter. After his experiences with Social Services, he decided to wait until he had a bit more to go on, or at least until his sergeant came back.

"Mr Macaulay, shall we start with you? Please wait here Miss Manover. One of us will be back shortly to see how you are and update you."

She just looked at him and said nothing, he didn't know how much she understood. But she knew and understood the click of the door locking when Matt & Jim left the room.

They went through to a small windowless room. In the middle of the room there was a plain table with a couple of chairs on either side. More chairs were stacked in a corner. A phone hung on the wall by the door, and some sort of recording device appeared bolted to the table.

"Worried it will be nicked?" Matt asked, as he sat down.

"You wouldn't believe what goes from here, I'd bolt the chairs down if I had my way."

I guess it's not meant to be nice, thought Matt as he looked around, it would be really grim if I was a criminal. It was now just gone one in the morning. He'd had a long day and then this unexpected trouble. He just wanted to get this interview over and done with and get to bed.

Luckily Jim seemed to feel the same way, and they started to make good progress recounting the night's events. Jim was pleased; Matt made a clear and exact witness, a rarity in Police work, especially witnessing a brawl outside a pub. This reinforced Jim's belief that Matt was what he claimed to be, a passer-by who simply stepped in to prevent a more serious event. They turned their heads at the soft knock on the door. It was Sarah, she handed Jim two sheets of paper.

"The searches you wanted." She fidgeted uneasily, and brushed her hair behind her ears. Jim started to look at the papers.

"Och they're fine..." She needed to keep his attention. "It's just that there is a man who says he wants to join your interview. He says he's a Met Police Officer on an ongoing case. It's most irregular and I don't like it, or him for that matter."

Jim was confused; it was not protocol to interrupt an interview unless you had good reason. How could anyone, let alone another copper from another force, know who he was interviewing? He didn't like it either. He considered for a moment. "Right, I will see him in the bosses' office. Can you contact the sarge and ask him to get back here as soon as he can? I will try and find out who we are dealing with."

Detective Inspector Nick Parson of the Metropolitan Police did not like being kept waiting. He considered it rude and ignorant for him to be kept hanging around in this draughty corridor. They didn't even have the common courtesy to show him into a waiting room. Not that he was a cheerful person to start with, but his mood had definitely turned sour. He didn't like Scotland, he didn't like having to deal with underlings and he didn't like being in this poxy excuse for a police station because his own staff had screwed up. What a mess. Parson had come in the back door of the station, he thought it would be more discreet that way and had hoped to slip in and out. Instead he was now stuck here in this glorified hallway, with peeling paint and dingy lighting. There were two doors off the corridor, one that the woman that he had spoken to had disappeared through and another one with a small frosted glass window. There was a light on in the room beyond. He tried the handle, it was locked. He heard someone move inside, then silence. That's her, he thought.

"The bitch," he muttered. Rattling the door handle, he liked the thought that he might be scaring her. His arrogance didn't allow him to worry; he just found it tedious that he had to become involved. The woman returned.

"PC Grey will see you now sir. Would you like to follow me?" She turned and held the door open for him and led him through the Operations room to some offices. The young officer stood up as he entered the room. Parson held out his hand and turned up the corners of his thin lips in a semblance of a smile.

"Good of you to see me, I know you must be busy and appreciate your making time for me."

Jim Grey wasn't fooled. You don't appreciate anything pal, he thought. It was like shaking hands with a slimy wet lettuce leaf. He took a second to examine the man standing in front of him. He was tall, over six feet, with blonde thinning hair that he had styled rather than just cut, in a way that would have looked better on a younger man. He wore an obviously expensive suit but it hung off his bony frame. He didn't look frail, more pointedly skinny. His sharp nose, thin pale lips and narrow eyes gave him a coldness that had an almost physical effect on those in his company. Jim could see why Sarah had taken an instant dislike to the visitor.

"Sit down, please sir. D'you want to tell me what this is about?"

"Erm, Yes, thank you." Parson was concentrating on being polite. He fiddled with the notebook and pencil that he held. Whilst moving them incessantly, he never actually opened the book. It was if he had it all rehearsed, thought Jim.

"I have an arrest warrant for Marieke Manover, whom I believe you have detained here. We can come to her in a moment. But I understand that a young man was assisting her, a Matt Macaulay? I am interested in their relationship and why he felt the need to put my two officers in hospital."

~~~
~~~

Chapter 5: The Interview

Against his better judgement but because of the man's rank, Jim allowed Inspector Parson to accompany him back into the interview room. The agreement was that Jim would lead and the Inspector would just witness the statement. Both men knew that this wasn't really going to happen. Jim just felt that it would help get things cleared up sooner. He was cross at his own misjudgement. He had believed Matt Macaulay and was upset at the possibility that he had got things so very wrong. He introduced Inspector Parson and tried to start back where they had left off, but there was now a completely different atmosphere in the room. He took a different tack.

"Matt, why don't you start from the top and explain what happened earlier to DI Parson please?" He offered a smile, but Matt was not amused. He breathed deeply, let out a tired sigh and resignedly began to tell his story again.

He had been talking for a couple of minutes when he became aware that neither officer was listening to him. He glanced from one to the other. What's going on here he wondered? Jim Grey was staring at the pieces of paper in his hand looking bewildered while Nick Parson was tapping his pen on his notebook cover, as if tapping out a tune. Infuriated, Matt sat back, and folded his arms.

"I am so sorry if I am boring you guys, if you're not interested I'll just go, shall I? 'Cos I certainly have somewhere better to be."

Jim Grey looked up, but didn't speak. He squinted, looking perplexed and lost for words. Parson sat up in his chair slowly. He deliberately placed his notebook and pen to one side, placing both palms flat on the table. He spread his fingers, and tapped them gently. Leaning forwards, he spoke softly:

"Look Matt, to be honest, I'm not really interested, because I don't buy a word of it. What I want to know is did you just get pissed off when you were caught trying to buy a screw, or had you arranged to meet her, and if so what are you two up to? Long way to bring a tart for a quick shag?"

He leaned back in his chair again. Matt's jaw dropped momentarily in disbelief, but he quickly regained his composure. Sitting up straighter, he stared hard at the Londoner.

"Firstly, you can address me as Mr Macaulay. Secondly, mind your fucking language. Thirdly, this is downright outrageous. What planet are you on?"

"What I call outrageous, Mr. Macaulay, is soliciting a prostitute with a child; aiding and abetting a known felon; perverting the course of justice; resisting arrest and assaulting two police officers in the course of their duty. And that's only to start with unless you start talking soon."

Parson raised his eyebrows as he finished the tirade. Matt thought that he looked almost as if he was enjoying himself. He turned to the Scottish constable.

"What policemen? You were there? They didn't identify themselves, did they? When do policemen go about attacking bairns and drugging young girls? Tarts or not."

"There were drugs involved?" Jim Grey spoke for the first time.

"The girl is a known user, they were probably hers," answered Parson, a little too quickly. "I'm more interested in why you think that just because you say that a policeman doesn't identify himself that gives you the right to put him in hospital?"

"I stopped them, no more, no less. If they were coppers, then policing in England is worse than I thought. Roll on Independence."

Matt couldn't understand why PC Grey was being so quiet, and looking so bewildered. He'd seemed ok to start with.

"Hang on, what's all this got to do with you anyway?" He continued, "You have no jurisdiction here."

"I'm simply assisting my Scottish colleague with his investigation, aren't I?" Parsons turned to Jim, but didn't quite get the answer he was looking for.

"Yes well, erm... this interview is being suspended for the time being. I need to gather more evidence and refer the matter to my superiors. There seems to be some glaring inconsistencies here." Jim folded the paper in his hand and stood up. Neither Matt nor Parson knew what he meant.

Matt really couldn't understand what was happening. He had been brought up to respect the law, in some circumstances previously, in the Marines, he had effectively been the law. He felt stupidly frustrated in the face of lies and ineptitude. He suspected there was more to the girl's story than she was letting on, but this was crazy, why was this man making such wild accusations? If she was running from him, he didn't blame her for keeping quiet. There had to be a way forward.

"Why not take some independent evidence?" he asked. "The Park Bar CCTV system. That's probably how they saw it and called the police. There's a screen behind the bar that shows the staff what is going on outside and around the building. They have a very expensive security system, so I'm told."

"I'll look into it," nodded Jim. "You are to wait here, while Inspector Parson and I investigate things further." He wasn't quite sure what he was going to say to Parson. Hoping that the Sergeant had returned, he politely suggested that the DI joined him in his boss's office.

Parson didn't like the initiative being taken away from him. He also wasn't keen that they got to the CCTV recording any time soon either. He certainly wasn't going to meekly follow this PC out of the room. "You go ahead, I'll join you in a minute. I need to catch up on the condition of my men in hospital." The two left Matt alone again. He began to realise why things were bolted down if this is how they treated people.

Returning to the Sergeant's office, Jim was very relieved to see his boss. He was about to launch into his account of what should have been a straightforward night when he caught sight of another man standing in the corner. "Not more brass," he thought, "that's all we need."

Sergeant Ron Harrison gave him a resigned smile. "Jim, this is Mr Murdo MacNeil. Special Branch has asked that we take his advice in our dealings with DI Nick Parson."

"Parson? Not Macaulay? But he's one of us," interrupted Jim, but somehow he wasn't surprised.

"No, he most certainly isn't. He's from the Met, and has no business running freelance round my city. Now do you want to tell me what's been going on, and why you look like a wet Sunday in Arbroath?"

Jim recounted the evening's events. Both men listened without interruption. "Parson claims that his men were trying to arrest Manover but I got Sarah to check and there is no warrant issued for her...anywhere! He also said that she is a known drug addict, well, again I don't know where he gets that from and there is absolutely nothing about her on file either here or in England."

"On the other hand," added MacNeil, "If you look him up, Matt Macaulay he has a glowing military record, while Parson's team is being investigated. I know who I would believe."

"So, what do we do now?" asked the Sergeant. But nobody got the chance to reply, as there was a knock on the door.

The policemen exchanged glances, but before anyone could say "Come in" the door opened and Parson stepped through.

"Ah, you must be Sergeant Harrison." He completely ignored Jim and held his hand out towards the Senior Officer. After a brief fingertip shake, he carried on.

"Look, I have just been on to my guys, there seems to have been a bit of a misunderstanding. It could well have been that my constable didn't identify himself properly. Evans is Welsh and hard to understand." He laughed at his own quip but nobody else in the room joined in the humour. "So, that may be why this girl took fright and this Macaulay lad may have thought he was up to no good. I suggest you warn him about excessive force and let him go. There is no real harm done."

Jim was open mouthed at Parson's complete change of tune. The other two made no response. He wondered if the Londoner now seemed less sure of himself and if it had anything to do with the presence of this MacNeil character. The silence just hung in the room.

Parson had no patience for these negotiating games and didn't like feeling out of control of the situation, especially over a stupid tart.

"If you have no questions then, I'll go and get my boys from casualty and we will get out of your way. Unless of course there is anything I can do to help?"

The Sergeant glanced at Jim, to ensure he remained silent.

"No, thank you, however I will need a statement from each of your officers regarding their actions tonight. Plus, documented reasons for your dropping the charges I believe you were mentioning earlier. Can you arrange a time to bring them in?"

"Yes of course, I will email you once I know when they will be fit to give a statement. They are after all, injured in the line of duty." With a slight nod of his head Parson turned and left the room.

Sergeant Harrison shook his head, and looked at Murdo. "I see what you mean." He sighed.

"Ok, let's go talk to Macaulay, and see if he will buy this plan of yours."

The three men went back to the interview room. Passing the operations room Jim saw Sarah. "How's the girl holding up?" he asked.

"She's OK, doesn't say much. I don't know if she understands what I am saying, or is just pretending. I have told her she needs to stay to verify Mr Macaulay's statement. She just nods and clutches that child and the bag. I offered her the baby facilities to change or feed him, but she refused."

"Thanks." Jim had to quicken his step to catch up with the others.

Matt was sitting with his head resting on his arms. He was exhausted, both mentally and physically. It seemed a life time ago that he kissed his family good bye and headed for the ferry. It felt like some sort of nightmare. His head pounded, his limbs ached. It had been a while since he had used physical force on anyone and he was now paying the price. He couldn't get his head around the Londoner, surely no one could believe him...but then, he was the Poileas...and well, he had been ill, and people can be funny about you after brain surgery. He knew that well enough. His musing was interrupted by the sound of footsteps in the corridor. Here we go again, he thought.

Matt sat back and stretched as the three men entered the room. He looked from one to the other. He was intending to appear nonchalant, but nearly fell off his chair when Murdo MacNeil walked into the room. It was all getting too bizarre, he couldn't even begin to comprehend what he was doing here. Jim Grey looked a lot happier than when he had left. He smiled at Matt as he pulled up a chair for the third man, whose body language indicated that he was in charge. Interestingly, there was there was no sign of the Londoner. Ok, time to play it cool, Matt told himself as he readjusted his seat. Offence is the best form of defence he decided as they all sat down in front of him.

"Didn't expect to see you here! I hope you are about to return the favour," he stared at Murdo who was pulling up a chair.

"No, actually, I am about to ask another one but I will let Sergeant Harrison explain."

The Sergeant started to give Parson's revised version of what happened, but Matt interrupted.

"No way! I am not in the habit of putting people in hospital over misunderstandings. They were attacking her and the kid. Where is he anyway? Was he spooked 'cos I mentioned the syringe or the CCTV? They were not trying to arrest her!" He was emphatic. "You go check out both and you'll see that I am right. That's probably what he's doing now, getting rid of evidence, while you're all sat here faffing." Frustrated, Matt rose to his feet, growled and shook his head.

"OK son, calm down, why don't you sit down again and we can try to sort this out."

Matt moodily kicked the chair, looked at it as if it had offended him and turned it around before he finally sat on it. He leant on the back rest and stared at the three men opposite. The Sergeant shot an "are you sure about this" look at Murdo, who then took the lead.

"We do believe you. Jim here did some checking and there is no arrest warrant issued either here or internationally for the girl. So, she is free to go. The men in hospital aren't going to press charges against you, so indeed you are free to go too. But as you said, there is more to this."

He turned to the other policemen. "Did I mention that we had met before?" he asked nodding in Matt's direction. "Yes, he helped me out on a very tricky situation on the side of a mountain."

Turning to Matt. "Do you remember I said that I'd been working for the Police in London? Or had you left by then?" He asked the question because Matt was staring at him blankly. He wasn't sure if the young man was being stroppy or really didn't know. He continued to explain further.

"Well one of the investigations was into human trafficking, mostly prostitution, some organ harvesting. It's a grim business. The Special Branch case was heading pretty close to home, so they asked for some discreet outside help, and that's me." He placed some photographs on the table. "Do you recognise any of these men?"

Matt looked at them. "Yes," he picked one up and handed it back to Murdo. "That's the Welsh creep who tried to grab the kid, and who now has a broken nose." He tapped another photo.

"And that's the thug with the syringe."

"They both work for Parson. Constable Rhydian Evans is on a Police exchange programme from Cardiff. Sergeant Malcolm Green is from Birmingham originally, but has worked with Parson for the last three years, he is known as a bit of a charmer, but not tonight, obviously. Their names keep cropping up in and around the investigation. Moreover, there has been a high level of assaults on women in their patch that they have been distinctly inept in solving. All a bit vague I know. But then they show up here trying to snatch this girl. I don't know what they are up to but I don't believe in coincidences either. Whatever the reason, I think they'll go for her again. They have come this far after all. I think they may leave it a couple of days and try again."

"Can't you protect her?" asked Matt.

"What from?" asked Harrison, "We have no evidence. Even in the unlikely event that she trusted us enough to make a complaint, it will take weeks to sort out and we have no grounds to hold her."

"I was following up on the two of them," said Murdo pointing at the mug shots on the table. "I didn't know how high or wide the problem went. I didn't know that Parson was involved until now. I need some time to tie it all together."

"So, what are you going to do now then? I take it you've let them go?" asked Matt. "Can't she just press charges for assault?"

Murdo glanced at his colleagues. “Well, that’s where these officers here are distinctly nervous. But I need a bit of help.” He paused and looked at Matt. Harrison was fiddling with his mobile phone, looking unconvinced. Jim Grey sat bolt upright, not quite believing what he was hearing. Matt returned his gaze, waiting for him to continue.

“At Christmas,” he continued “you were saying that you needed a bit of purpose, something to do that used your skills and training?”

“No, that’s what my mother was saying. All that is behind me now as you probably know if you have looked at my records, and if you’re asking me favours without at least Googling me ... I really want nothing to do with you, I never did like half arsed plans.”

Murdo smiled. “Yes, it did say somewhere that you could be a stubborn bastard, but it also said that you are a completer finisher, could be relied upon to see a job through. What was the point of you saving her this evening, to let them grab her again and do God knows what tomorrow? They will get at her again, before she has time to press charges.”

Matt pursed his lips and breathed in and out deeply. Murdo was right and he knew it but he didn’t like the feeling that he was being sucked into something...but then again, I did throw the first punch, he thought.

“What do you want me to do?”

“Miss,” Murdo paused, “Manover is it?” Jim nodded.

“Knows nobody, and has no reason to trust anyone in this city apart from you perhaps. All I am asking is, that you suggest to her that she leaves with you...invite her for breakfast or something; stay with her and keep her safe and out of the way for a couple of days, while I sort this out. That’s all. You can liaise with Jim here. You never know, if you gain her trust she may even tell you something that will help clear it all up. Just a day or so? Parson’s boys don’t know Glasgow, it’s just a precaution really, but there is the kid to consider too. Again, I’m not sure why, but I have a feeling in my bones that it would be good for us all if she didn’t disappear.”

Matt thought about this. He didn’t entirely trust Murdo. Would he be protecting Marieke or keeping tabs on her for him? Bit of both he thought. Why should he care? He could just walk away and go to bed; this was nothing to do with him after all. He wasn’t normally impulsive, but then remembered holding the little boy and the scared voice asking for his help. How could he explain to his family that he walked away and left them? His mother and sisters would never forgive him. Iona would worry about the kid, Kate would want the story, and his mother would just give him one of her looks. What choice did he have?

~~~
~~~

Chapter 6: Early Tuesday Morning: On the Run

Marieke looked up; there was a noise in the corridor. There must be people outside the door again. She had been dozing and was not sure how long they had been sitting there. The boy was laid across two seats, sleeping more soundly with his head resting on his mother's leg. All Marieke knew was that she was tired, stiff and very scared. It had been so long since she had been home. The sad thing was that there was nowhere safe now that she could call home or where she would wish to be. Nor was there anyone she could trust to help her. That woman had stayed with her for a while and chatted. Marieke did understand a little, but it was meaningless. All she wanted to know was when she could get out of here and carry on running. She held her breath as the door opened, then exhaled a long, slow sigh of relief as Matt walked through the door. He had helped, but would probably be going now.

He sat down next to her and smiled. She smiled back. She still had his jacket around her shoulders, he had forgotten about it.

"They say we can go."

"All OK?"

"Yes, would you like to go and find some breakfast?"

"Huh?"

"Food?"

"Yes, Where?"

"I dunno, my hotel?"

"Hotel? You want sex!" She sounded disgusted and disappointed.

"No, why would you think that?"

"Hotel, Sex... No! I leave now."

"No, wait.... listen."

Gathering her bag and lifting the child onto her shoulder, Marieke turned, tears of anger, desperation and disappointment in her eyes.

Matt raised his voice, equally exasperated, "No Sex!! For God's sake!"

She paused, not knowing where to go or what to do. Who could she trust?

"Wait!" holding up his hand, he suddenly had a brain wave. When he had been in Poland climbing a couple of years ago he had set up a translation app on his smart phone.

"You speak Polish?"

She gestured with her fingers, "A little, you?"

"I can...watch this!"

Marieke shifted the weight of the child in her arms and watched him type something into his phone, and then he handed it to her. It took a second to work out, and then she read in Polish:

"Bad men no like you," She nodded, so he took the phone and he typed again.

"Bad men no like me either." She gave a knowing smile and nodded. He took the phone once more.

"We go to hotel to hide until they go. Rest, eat and be safe?"

Marieke thought about this. He had saved her. What did she have to lose? She smiled tentatively and nodded.

"Ok?" asked Matt.

"Ok," she agreed.

"And no sex!!"

"Ok," Marieke laughed. It was odd, but despite the desperate situation, she hadn't felt quite so safe or even been able to laugh in a long time.

As they stepped outside the station, Marieke was struggling with her bag and the child. Matt offered to take the bag from her, but she became quite defensive and gave him the little boy to hold instead. He thought that odd, he couldn't imagine either of his sisters doing that. Thinking of his sisters, he would have to call Iona tomorrow and explain. Perhaps they could go and pick up the car after all as it was to be fitted with a child seat.

It did not surprise Matt that a taxi was waiting, it had probably been called by MacNeil. They climbed in and sat back into the seat, and finally began to relax as Matt gave directions to his hotel.

They were nearly there. The taxi stopped at red lights on Argyle Street, minutes away from sleep thought Matt. He didn't care that he was giving the bed to Marieke and her son. He could sleep on a clothes line right now and had almost dozed off in the cab. His gentle dozing was abruptly interrupted by Marieke jabbing him sharply in the thigh. He opened his eyes, feeling vaguely annoyed. He first thought was that Marieke was pointing at their hotel, but then he focussed. Just past the main entrance to the hotel there was a boarded up coffee shop doorway and loitering in the shadows were two familiar figures huddling against the cold. One was talking on a phone, the other looking up the street. He couldn't see their faces, but it was definitely them.

"What the hell!" exclaimed Matt. How had they got there? Some people might have panicked at this point, but for him, although it had been a while, the training kicked in. He felt his car keys in his pocket. He lent forward to the driver.

"Listen pal; change of plan. Take the next right to the NCP car park." He turned to Marieke.

"We'll take my car to another hotel." She just looked blank and scared. He squeezed her hand. "Don't worry, I have a plan."

As he paid the driver, he also managed to buy the man's hat from him. It was the most expensive baseball cap he had ever bought. He knew the drill now. He carried the boy and Marieke hefted her bag as they found the little red Nissan. They sat in the car, as Matt used his phone again to explain his plan. He handed her the device so that she could read his message.

"We go to my sister's house. She investigates things and helps people. It's a long way from here. Safe."

Marieke nodded slowly, she was not sure now. Would she ever be able to get away from them? She did not want to endanger more people. But right now, she had no choice.

Matt then called Kate, aware that he would be waking her up.

Alarmed to be receiving a call before dawn, she immediately thought there was something wrong at home. He quickly assured her that there wasn't, but keeping details to the minimum, asked her if he and a friend could come and stay...that morning. Due to her own sensitivities, she did not want to discuss her location on the phone, so they agreed to meet at the "large supermarket in town." Only the two of them knew it was the Morrison's in Fort William.

To get to the motorway out of town, they were going to have to follow the one-way system round Argyle Street, which would take them to the junction outside the hotel where their pursuers would be standing watching. They could drive straight by, but then again, they might stop right in front of them at the lights. He realised the limitations of using his phone to translate more than simple sentences, as he had to resort to demonstrating to Marieke that he wanted her and Kazik to lie on the floor so that he could cover them with a blanket.

Finally, Matt pulled the recently purchased, stained baseball cap down to cover as much of his hair and face as he could, and they set off into the traffic. Despite the early hour, the volume of cars and trucks was quite high, so progress was slow on the main road. As they crawled up to the hotel, Matt could see the two policemen still waiting. He had a better view of them as he crawled past. They were paying more attention to the pavements and side streets, than to the traffic on the main road. One had a hand held camera type device. The Nissan was registered in his sister's married name, so he hoped that the connection to him would not be immediately obvious if they were scanning cars as they passed. The smaller wiry man looked a bit odd wearing dark glasses and his nose looked painfully misshapen. The larger one had a hat on, under which a dressing was just visible. Both looked thoroughly miserable, but determined. What have I got myself into, thought Matt. These are serious people, who have access to resources and are not going to give up...but then again, neither will I.

The traffic cleared and they made their way out of the city without any trouble. Not knowing whether Parson and his men had further look outs, or cars touring, looking for them, Matt didn't take the hat off or tell Marieke that she could get up from the floor until they had crossed the Erskine Bridge over the river Clyde. Even then he was quite pleased when, cuddling the child, she chose simply to lie on the back seat and sleep. Looking at her in the rear view mirror, she looked smaller and delicate. The tension and cool hardness had left her face, and her whole demeanour softened. Her light brown hair, although dirty, was short and wispy around her face. She had a small nose and a dimple on her chin. Her clothes were dirty too. Stained and ill-fitting as well as inappropriate. Is that all she has? He wondered. There couldn't be all that much in the precious bag she carried. Despite everything, he couldn't help but think that she had something about her. Bet she scrubs up OK... he thought, and then chided himself for being such an idiot.

They had just passed the famous Green Welly, and were heading across Rannoch Moor into Glen Coe as dawn began to break. Kazik woke before his mother on the back seat. He wasn't crying exactly, more moaning to himself than anything. Obviously unhappy, but not really expecting any relief or help. Matt put some music on, not so much to drown him out, but on the off chance that it might soothe him. He's probably hungry, he thought.

"Been a long night for both of us mate," he commented out loud. The sound of his voice disturbed Marieke who woke with a start. She instinctively held her child more tightly, and stared wide eyed around her. Matt glimpsed her haunted expression, it was as if she had woken up and then remembered how terrified she was. As she sat up, the survivor had returned.

The mountains glowed with a pink golden mist as the sun slowly rose between the peaks. It gave the steep sided valley a magical feel, worlds away from the terror and violence of the night before. Marieke whispered something in the child's ear as she stared out of the window. She turned him around so that he could see the view. She caught Matt's eye in the mirror. "Beautiful," she smiled, pointing at the window.

"Yes", he responded. "That's the Lost Valley on your left and the Aonach Eagach Ridge on your right... I've walked that..." But she wasn't really listening, just staring, enchanted by the awesome view.

They passed a couple of camper vans parked up, no doubt full of sleeping climbers, but saw very few other cars on the road. Consequently, it wasn't long before they were winding their way into the outskirts of Fort William.

"We meet my sister now," Matt reminded Marieke, speaking slowly.

She nodded and he was relieved to be understood.

It had started to drizzle as they turned at the roundabout into the supermarket car park. Matt instinctively scanned the few parked cars. They were empty. He shook his head. Don't be paranoid Macaulay, they couldn't be waiting for you here, he thought as he drove around slowly. He began to tut as he couldn't see Kate either. The morning was dreich. The mist dripped off deserted trolleys, and puddles of dark water obscured the parking lines. By the side of the shop seagulls pecked at the discarded remains of an unwanted take away. Somebody had tried to be sick in a bin and missed. It all seemed so bleak after the magnificence of the mountains.

After a moment he spotted Kate standing by the bus shelter, huddled against the timetable. Her hood was up, scarf around her face and her hands deep in the pockets of her blue duffel coat, protecting herself from the elements. He stopped and leaned over to open the car door. She got into the front, beside him.

"What's going on?" Iona's going to go spare...you haven't got her new car!"

"That's the least of my worries," he nodded towards the back seat.

Kate saw the young woman and child for the first time. Noting Marieke's clothes, her mind raced trying to work out what on earth Matt had got himself into.

"Your friends?" She asked.

Matt nodded a response.

"I knew it was trouble, when you rang in the middle of the night. Let's get back to mine, and you can start explaining."

"I wish I could," he sighed.

Kate directed Matt back up the dual carriageway, into a meandering housing estate on the hill side, overlooking the sea. He asked how long it had taken her to walk down, as she didn't seem that damp considering the morning mist. She explained that there was a short cut, a path leading through the woods from behind the houses that came out at the train station.

"Easy going down, but hard work climbing back up after the pub," she laughed.

The house had a traditional Victorian frontage, but inside had been completely renovated and contained every mod con.

"This is swish," admired Matt as they came through a spacious hall into a large dazzlingly light kitchen. The entire eastern wall had been replaced with a large window/patio door which led out onto a spacious balcony. Kate asked Matt if he and Marieke were "together", to which he assured her that they were not. She was not surprised, but even more confused. She suggested that they rested, got washed and changed, then they could have some breakfast and he could enlighten her as to what was going on. Matt used his phone to explain this briefly to Marieke.

"Do you have any clean clothes?" Kate asked.

"Him yes, me no," answered Marieke in her limited English, pointing to her son.

"And I left mine in the hotel room we couldn't go back to." Matt chipped in.

Kate looked, from one to the other bemused. "OK, I'm sure you are going to explain all this to me in a bit. Meanwhile, I'll raid Janice and Bob's wardrobe and see if they have left anything you can borrow." She found jeans and a jumper that looked about Marieke's size but could only produce an extra-large T shirt for Matt which he declined saying. "Don't worry; I'll grab something in town later." How long is he planning to stay for? She thought.

Although they were exhausted, none of them could rest, so in about an hour they were back around the kitchen table with coffee and croissants. Kazik was eating his, sitting on the floor, looking out the patio window. He seemed to be enjoying both the view and leaving sticky finger marks on the glass.

Marieke looked cleaner and at least a bit more refreshed. That's an improvement thought Matt. She was hardly recognisable as the girl in the alley from the night before.

Matt explained as best he could, what had happened to them. Some of it still didn't make sense to him, let alone to Kate. He tried to involve Marieke in the explanation, but apart from nodding every now and again she offered no further details.

Kate spoke slowly. "So, you are Polish?"

"No...Romanian."

"But... You read Polish on my Phone?" Matt butted in, showing her his handset.

"Yes, I talk a little Polish."

"I don't have a Romanian app!"

Kate was thinking; she distractedly played with the plate of pastries and rolls, picking up crumbs and eating them.

"You came from Romania to Glasgow?" Kate emphasised her questions gesturing with her hands, the movement from one place to another.

"No, London. Then Bus, from London to Glasgow." She bit her lip, stared down at her plate. How could she begin to explain what had happened to her? Would they believe her, could she trust them? What else could she do? She had to think.

Her thoughts were interrupted. "But you knew the men who attacked you and the man called Parson." It wasn't a question, but a statement from Kate. Marieke said nothing, she couldn't. Kazik was cooing happily, now drawing shapes on the window with his fingers. Marieke spoke to him sharply. He turned and looked at her resentfully.

"Come on wee man, I'll wash your hands." Matt got up to attend to the child. Kate leaned over and picked up his phone. She fiddled for a moment, then found the translation app and typed. She pushed the handset across the table towards the Marieke who read: "If you want us to help, you have to tell us what is going on."

"Soon." Kate emphasised. Marieke shrugged, she was confused, and it had been a long time since anyone had offered to help her. But what should she do?

Sensing her turmoil, Kate changed the subject. "Ok then," she smiled. "Let's go play." She led them out of the kitchen, down some steps into a large garden. There was a diamond shaped lawn, bordered with spring flowers, bushes nestled against the high fence. A path led down beside the lawn to the far end of the garden, where behind some shrubs was an old wooden gate.

"This takes us to the cut through the woods," she told them, as she opened the gate. They were high above the town. Matt could see all the way down to the supermarket car park where they had met earlier. He could see the train and bus stations with stooped miserable looking commuters starting their journey to work. He seemed to have lost track of time, it was still early in the morning. The rain had stopped, but it was still damp under foot. Suddenly there was a clearing. Strangely, in the middle of nowhere, on the side of a hill, the council some years back had decided to build a play park. There were swings, a slide, a climbing frame and various tunnels, all brightly painted. Marieke just stood and looked at them. She had not understood why they were leaving the house, and had never really seen a park like this. Matt took Kazik out of her arms and ran with him to the top of the slide. The little boy shrieked with laughter as they slid down, and was already keen to climb up and go again. Kate sat on one of the swings, gently rocking back and fro. Soon mother and son were playing together. Matt joined his sister on the swings.

"What's the script?" He asked.

"The way I see it, she obviously knew those blokes, but she is confused and scared and not going to talk to us now, even if she could. What we need to do is build up some trust so that she will. So, we relax here for a bit, do the normal stuff like shopping, going for coffee, eating, chatting, and then see what happens."

"But how is she going to tell us?"

"Ah I have a plan for that. I use a programme called Language Line to translate foreign documents, articles and stuff. I'll show her how to use it, so that we can ask what the boy likes to eat, that sort of thing. Then later, see if she will have a go, to tell us what's going on. It's probably going to be all very boring, but you need to be able to get Iona's car, not to mention your stuff from that hotel, without being chased by thugs."

"That would be good."

"Murdo had no business getting you involved in this."

"To be fair, I kinda got myself involved, outside the Park Bar. I would like to see their CCTV recording, if it hasn't been destroyed by now."

"You just want to see yourself being an action hero," she teased.

Kate looked across the park. Marieke and Kazik were on the roundabout. He was on her lap while she was gently pushing it with her foot. She was singing to him, and he was smiling. They could be any young family anywhere, she thought, not two fugitives on the run.

Unfortunately, the tranquillity was brought to an abrupt end by a sudden quickening in the breeze as large drops of rain began to fall, and broke the spell. They all ran back to the house.

Kate made hot chocolate. They all laughed when Matt got squirty cream on his nose, which Kazik then copied. As they sipped their drinks Kate opened her laptop and sat next to Marieke. The Language Line programme opened showing two boxes. Kate set it to translate from English to Romanian. She typed into the left hand box:

"This will translate for us better than Matt's phone."

She pressed the "translate" icon and the sentence immediately appeared in the right hand box in Romanian. Marieke smiled and nodded. Kate continued:

"This is where I live. Would you like to stay with me for a couple of days, until the men who were chasing you go away? Or would you like to go somewhere else?"

Kate didn't just want to follow Murdo's plan. By giving Marieke a choice she was sure she would find out more. Marieke paused after she read it. Giving a slight smile she nodded slowly. Kate offered her the key board. Firstly, she just looked at it, and then very slowly she typed:

"Yes, thank you, just one day or two, until I think what to do."

It was Kate's turn to nod. As Kazik watched cartoons on TV and Matt dozed in the chair, slowly but surely the two young women began to converse. Kate established that Kazik was eighteen months old, what he would eat and that he was probably in need of nappies and clothes. It had been a couple of days since she had left London, so did not have much of anything left for the child in her bag. Marieke didn't have any money, but hoped to earn some when her "trouble was over". Kate offered to put her in contact with the Eastern European community in Fort William, but she was not keen on that idea. The conversation was kept light and child focussed so that Marieke did not feel threatened. It seemed to be working. Marieke asked about Matt; did he live in Glasgow? Was he married? Kate couldn't help but smile. No matter what, her brother always aroused interest with the ladies. She explained that he lived on a small island off the West Coast of Scotland, but this didn't mean much to Marieke. Maybe they would get a map out for her later.

By lunch time the rain had passed so they decided that they would go shopping. Marieke was concerned by her own lack of money, but Kate managed to reassure her that there were some basic things that she could not do without.

Marieke couldn't help but grow to like the brother and sister. She kept looking for the catch. How they were going to deceive and use her as everyone else had, but she couldn't find it. She had noticed the long scar, like a zip up the back of his neck and skull and understood that something bad must have happened to him too. Perhaps he would understand. At the moment, she had little choice but to stay with them. Parson had caught up with her when she had run off by herself before. As much as she hated to admit it, she needed help.

The other thing that truly amazed her was the change in Kazik. He had screamed at everyone, all the time in London. But here he was laughing and playing with Matt. He seemed to be able to distinguish between the good and bad people. She resolved to follow her son's instincts, but needed to work out how to resolve her troubles.

Fort William was not a big place, but despite the fact that the main shopping area had been left depleted by the ongoing recession, the shopping trip was a success. They drove back down to the Morrison's where they had started that morning; with the lights on, it looked less bleak. Matt put Kazik in a trolley and pushed him round the shop making brmm, brmm noises much to the child's amusement, while the girls stocked up on essentials. They then headed along the high street. Between the Lidl's store and a couple of charity shops they were able to buy a change of clothes and reasonable outdoor coats and boots. The tourist shops amused and amazed Marieke. There were so many things that she wanted to ask questions about, she even tried to use the app on Matt's phone to ask about the different tartans on sale. But most communicating was done through sign language, miming and laughing.

Although it was officially the beginning of summer, the tourist season had not really started yet, and the town was quiet. Matt didn't mind this. It would have been harder to keep an eye on things in a crowd. They popped into an arts and crafts shop and coffee bar owned by a friend of Kate's called Lorna Campbell and had some well earned cake. The shop was full of homemade novelties, designed and produced with wit and skill. Feeling more relaxed now, Matt bought some presents for Iona; a small pair of amber earrings for her and a rattle for the baby. You could have items personalised, so he had the name "Pumpkin" etched on it. He felt he would probably need a peace offering for delaying the return of her new car and thought that would make her smile. He knew she would understand when he explained. Neither he nor Kate had mentioned phoning home to explain what was happening.

"What could they say?" He asked himself. Also, while he was fairly sure that the danger was probably over now, he still felt the fewer people who knew where Marieke was the better. He didn't even intend to tell Murdo where they were until he understood a bit more about what was going on.

By the time, they got back up the hill to Kate's house the lack of sleep and stress was beginning to catch up with them. The conversation had become subdued, and for Matt at least thinking was becoming hard work. There was no argument when it was suggested that they all have an early dinner followed by an early night.

After they had eaten and Marieke settled her son to sleep, she returned to the kitchen. Matt sat next to her, opening his sister's lap top. He opened the translation page and typed.

"We need to talk about what happened to us last night."

She looked at him, clasping her hands together tightly in her lap, she slowly, resignedly, nodded.

He smiled reassuringly and continued typing:

"I am really tired and have to sleep. Why don't you just sit here by yourself and type up whatever you feel you can tell me? Kate will be here, but neither of us will pressure you. Then tomorrow we can talk about it. OK?"

He stood up, tousled her hair, turned and left the room, hugging his sister in the doorway. He was ready for some well earned rest, but he was content that they would get things sorted in the morning. Kate made some tea and handed Marieke a mug. She was just sitting, staring at the screen, lost in her own thoughts. Kate leaned past her and typed.

"I am in the living room watching TV if you need me."

She hugged Marieke's shoulders, took her own tea and left the room.

Marieke sat for ten minutes by herself before she realised she was crying. What should she say? Where would she start? Could she really share her living hell? Then she remembered Kazik laughing today and smiled through her tears. She couldn't remember seeing him laugh like that in a long time. This had to end, if only for him. She could not bear him suffering the same pain, fear and despair that she had. She pulled her chair forward and straightened her back. She was only able to type with two fingers, but she'd made up her mind to tell her story and was determined to see it through to the end, no matter how tired she was.

Kate popped her head round the door a couple of times to see if she was OK, but the girl was obviously lost in her own world and focussed on her task. It was well after midnight when Marieke came into the living room; her eyes were red and her pupils wide as if she had just relived a nightmare.

"I finished, I sleep now." She gave a deep sigh, waved wearily and left.

Kate walked over to the lap top. "Bloody hell, there's pages of it." As much as she wanted to read it, she knew that she was not in a fit state to take it in either. She pressed translate, and set the printer to produce two copies and went to bed.

Kate was sound asleep within five minutes. But three hours later when her phone started ringing she thought that she had only been asleep for a few minutes. First of all she thought she was dreaming, reliving Matt's early morning call of the night before, but it didn't stop. This can't be him; he's in bed, this couldn't be happening two nights in a row, could it? It was still ringing. She finally rolled over and groggily pulled the phone to her ear.

"What...this better be good...."

"Kate? Kate, is that you? It's Lorna; Lorna Campbell." Kate was wide awake now. Her friend's voice was wired. She was speaking quickly, in a terrified high pitch whisper.

"Yes, what's wrong? Talk slowly *math tha.*" Lorna took a deep breath, but didn't talk much more slowly.

"I don't know what's wrong, but I think you and your brother are in trouble. I have just had the Police here, at this time of night. They are from London and had somehow traced the fact your brother used his bank card in my shop today. They say he and the girl are dangerous fugitives and they are searching for them here in town."

"*Mac na galla*"... "Son of a bitch," swore Kate.

~~~
~~~

CHAPTER 7: Early Wednesday Morning:

Kate listened to her friend tell of her shock and fear at being woken in the middle of the night by the English Police; not doubting that there must be some sort of danger for them to disturb her so late. Unfortunately, she had told them that Matt and Kate were siblings, but thankfully she did not know where Kate was staying.

On ending the call Kate closed her eyes and took a deep breath. Her mind was racing. This couldn't be happening; they could be at her door any second. In one sense, it all seemed a bit farfetched. She knew about police corruption, she knew about fascist thugs, but the police didn't usually behave quite like this. Chasing the girl was one thing, but scaring people and saying that she was in danger was ridiculous. She shivered and went to the window, feeling daft peering out of the side of the curtain, but with a sickening sense of dread growing in her stomach. The street was dark. Ok, we have a few minutes, she thought as she went to wake Matt.

Barely suppressing her fear, she ran to his room and shook Matt roughly. He groaned and turned over.

"Matt wake up," she hissed sharply, shaking him again and turning the bedside light on.

"What?" he groaned, squinting his eyes at the brightness.

"They're here! Here in Fort William. Looking for you and telling people you are dangerous.

They could spot the Nissan in the drive and be here any second."

Wide awake now, Matt sat up. He could hear the panic in her voice, but couldn't quite grasp what was happening. "What's gone off? Start from the top and take it slowly."

Trying to stop herself shaking, Kate retold what Lorna had said. "Two Poileas, called Green and Evans woke her up at one o'clock this morning. They said that they were chasing two dangerous criminals and had been alerted to one of them using a credit card in her cafe. They said they had to call so late because the child and anyone you were with could be in danger. She told them that I couldn't be in danger as I was your sister." She paused. "Come to think of it, they will probably be heading for my old flat in Glen Nevis, nobody knows I'm here, there is no official record of it. They told her Marieke had some hold over you, and you both had to be found. The thing is, I think she believed him."

Matt thought for a moment. He could have kicked himself for using the card. He knew

Parson and his men were dangerous, but hadn't realised just how well connected they were. He had an idea. "What time is the next boat to Uist?"

"Huh? You lost it or something?"

"No, listen; this is what we are going to do. We leave the Nissan in any drive on the estate. I'll take Marieke and Kazik down the back way to the station, where we'll get the next train to Kyle, then jump on a coach to Uig, I'm sure the timetables are set up to meet the ferry. We'll hide on Uist. You go back to Glasgow in your car, find Murdo or Jim Grey, tell them what's happened and get help. Even if they do work out where we've gone, we will have a head start." He paused, thinking again. "Can you type this and do the translation thing for Marieke. You'd better wake her, she may freak if I do. Also, I'll need cash, can you pick me some up from the machine and drive by the station and give it to me on your way out of town?"

If Marieke was surprised that Parson's men had caught up with them again, but she did not show it. In truth, she had seen how ruthless they could be, so nothing they did surprised her really. She simply nodded resignedly when she read the sheet of paper Kate handed her, and started to gather her few belongings together. Marieke reacted strangely when Kate tried to help pack her baby bag, snatching the bag from her, and muttering something in her own tongue. Perhaps she feels fed up and let down, thought Kate.

Few words were spoken as they prepared. It was not long before they were ready. Matt now had a rucksack filled with all he believed to be essential. He did not know how long they would have to hide for, but he felt better prepared. He had everything from baby food to firelighters. He offered to Marieke that he could take some of her belongings, but she refused. Kazik thankfully slept through the whole proceedings, wrapped snugly in his new all in one snow suit.

Kate hugged Marieke and Matt at the back gate of the house, just as they were about to go their separate ways.

"Hang on" she whispered urgently, "You've forgotten something". She ran back into the house and grabbed the half dozen sheets of paper from the printer. She came running back and thrust them into a side pocket on Matt's bag. "It's what Marieke wrote last night, could be important." At that they parted. Matt, carrying Kazik, led Marieke down the hill by torch light, while Kate went to move cars. The plan was to meet at the railway station in half an hour.

Kate was beginning to get worried. Now driving her own black Mazda, she had stopped at a cash machine then driven past the train station and around the one way system three times, but there was still no sign of Matt and Marieke. They were twenty minutes late. Had something happened? Had one of them slipped? Had Parson's men caught up with them? Not one to usually worry, she began to feel sick with fear. After all Matt had been through, for him to be hurt by some sleaze ball was unthinkable. She hated feeling this helpless and not knowing what to do. He had said not to call him so she would drive around one more time, then she might just have to. It was still dark and damp, the car lights glistened off the wet road, and the street lamps seemed to have a fuzzy sort of sparkle. The gaps between the buildings and doorways were filled with dark shadows that she could not see into. They could be hiding, she thought and they might not be alone.

As she passed the station again, heading towards the town centre. She saw an odd single light flash ahead on the pavement and then go off. Seconds later the same thing happened again. Can it be a bike? Of course not, it's Matt's torch. She pulled over to where she thought the light had been, and began to drive along the curb slowly. Quickly and quietly Matt and Marieke emerged from the shadows. She stopped ready to hand them the money. Instead, both of them got into the car.

"Drive" he said. "Round to the Gleaner Garage."

"What's wrong? I've been worried sick."

"Didn't you see them? They are at the train station. We'll never get past them."

"No, I didn't see anyone. I wouldn't recognise them anyway."

"That's true, and they wouldn't recognise you."

"What are you thinking Matt?" His sister knew that tone.

"Change of plan. We'll drive to the ferry and you get the train to Glasgow."

Kate groaned as she pulled up by the petrol station and looked at her watch. "Does that mean you are going to throw me out here?" Given the circumstances, she couldn't think of a valid reason to object. But she wasn't relishing the walk in the rain.

"We have a head start on them, and they don't know you, this car or where any of us are going. Take the path back up to the house and go down for the train with the morning commuters. I'll leave the car at Uig Pier."

"Well you'd better look after it!!" she sighed.

Matt took her hand. "Love you. Be careful. Just get to Glasgow and find Murdo."

"You too," She smiled. "We are going to have to get this sorted, 'cos never mind Parson, Iona's going to kill you."

“Maybe we should set Iona on him, he wouldn’t stand a chance then!” he said. “But we have no choice now, this is the safest way. I know it sounds mad, but they followed us here, so let’s just get on with it eh?”

They were parked at the side of the garage forecourt. The security lights illuminated the road as Kate reluctantly got out allowing Matt to take the driving seat. She still had that knot in her stomach as she watched the Mazda’s tail lights disappear into the distance.

~~~
~~~

Chapter 8: Wednesday morning commuting.

Kate pulled up her hood as she watched her brother drive off. She tucked her hair back as far as she could. Looking around she headed toward the cut for the path up the hill. She wasn't scared of Parson and his goons, they were not after her. She was more annoyed at them for being responsible for her traipsing around in the rain, two nights in a row. She was walking into the wind, the drizzle soaking her face, obscuring her vision. The path was sodden under foot, and slippery beneath her suede dolly shoes. Not dressed for hiking, she missed her footing and stumbled forward, into a muddy puddle. She cursed under her breath, and swore that she would bill them for new shoes too when this was all sorted out.

The moon shone an eerie light through the clouds, by which she could see the outline of the play park up ahead. It was still a climb away, but eventually she made it. Breathing deeply, she paused at the swings. There was no point rushing now, she couldn't get much wetter. Looking round, it seemed odd that only a few hours ago, they were making their plans, not expecting to be chased into the night. Reflecting on her earlier panic, it wasn't just that Lorna was freaking, Parson and his men did seem to exude a sinister air of menace. They certainly spooked Matt, and that wasn't easily done.

How were they going to sort it out?

Marieke's translation, of course. Kate found new energy, her copy was on the kitchen table, and she needed to read it and the sooner the better. Now was as good a time as any.

Finally, back at the house, she peeled off her wet clothes and poured herself a coffee. She had intended to have a shower and change, but started reading the sheets of paper on the table, then couldn't stop. The true scale of Matt and Marieke's predicament gradually became very clear to her. It wasn't that she hadn't believed Matt when he explained his reasons for wanting to hide from Parson, but even if only half of it was true, Marieke's account made it clear that it was not simply a matter of hiding from him; the man had to be stopped. If it was all true, he was a very dangerous individual. Making sure that she still had a soft copy, Kate folded the pages into her bag and got herself ready. She had a train to catch.

Dawn brought light, but no warmth to Fort William train station. There was only one car in the whole car park. It sat, cold and desolate, with the windows covered in condensation. There was definitely no warmth emanating from the two men inside it.

"I can't believe there is nowhere in this dump to get coffee, how far did you go?" Evan's nasal whine, through his painfully broken nose, made him even more unintelligible than usual. He swallowed pain killers with some flat warm cokc that had been in the car too long. His bruised face showed his distaste. "I also can't believe," he continued, gesticulating with the empty bottle, "that he's had us sit here for half the night. Where's the sense in that?"

"He had it in his head that they would try and make some sort of run for it after I spoke with the cafe owner. She could have warned the sister. Well, she should have done after I put the fear of God into her," he chuckled recalling the pleasant memory. "From here we can see the train, bus station and the main road out of town. No red Nissan and no tarts with their brats running for the post train or early bus.... but I did notice the black Mazda that drove round several times when I was having a walk, did you see it?"

"Yeah, but it's not them, it was driven by a woman. Too posh looking to be our girl." Evans was usually sharper than this, but he was cold and in pain.

"Interesting though, wanna see if you can Google any pictures of the sister?"

"Ok, but turn the car engine on again, it's frigging freezing."

There were more vehicles in the car park by 07.30. Evans had found several photos of Kate Macaulay by the time she walked into the station to catch the Glasgow train.

"Leave this to me," smiled Green putting on his gloves. "You look so bad you'll scare her away."

"What you gonna do?"

"Charm her! Make her think I am on her side."

He meant to smile, but even to Evans it looked like a leer.

Kate had walked to the far end of the station by the time Malcolm Green caught up with her. He flashed his warrant card at the guard who opened the turnstile allowing him access to the platform. She was obscured behind a pillar, but he could see the blue duffle coat and a satchel. He sensed that she was aware of his presence and watching him approach.

"Nice and easy," he thought.

"Excuse me, Miss Macaulay?"

There was no answer. Kate simply turned her head and looked him up and down, from his coppers shoes to the woollen hat, pulled down over his ears. Hostility oozed from every one of her pores. She was weighing up the situation, her glare challenging him to speak again.

Then he had a brain wave.

"Please don't be alarmed Miss Macaulay, I'm Jim Grey; here to help. Are you and Matt ok?"

Kate audibly breathed out, her muscles relaxed as a look of relief crossed her face.

"I'm on my way to Glasgow to find you, what are you doing here?"

"When we realised they'd traced Matt and the girl, I was sent to well, support you. Where is he?"

"They've gone to Uist." Kate could see that the policeman looked confused. "We know you said to stay around Glasgow, but he felt it just wasn't safe. They have the evidence you need; he just wanted to be out of the way while it's getting sorted."

"That's good, but where did you say?" Green had no idea where she meant, but knew he had to find out.

"South Uist," she repeated, but sensed that something was wrong. This guy was looking at her as if she had said Outer Mongolia, or somewhere on Mars. Another thing started to bother her. She was sure Matt had said that Jim Grey was a Glaswegian. In fact, she then recalled that he had described him as a "little, fat, Glaswegian." This guy was fat, but not little and he did not have a Scottish accent.

A lot of Scots don't know the Uists, but she was sure that Matt and Jim had talked. There was also that hat; it was pulled down at an odd angle. She regretted having told him anything. She looked at her watch; the train would be here any second.

"Sorry, erm, can I see your warrant card?"

"Yes of course," Smiled Green. "It's in the car. Why don't you come over with me, out of the cold and I will get it for you?" As he turned gesturing towards the car park, his hat rose slightly over his right ear. Kate caught the glimpse of something white, a bandage or a dressing? The penny dropped. He went to say something else, but was drowned out by a station announcement and the whoosh and noise of the approaching train. She listened as the doors opened and people began to board. Being at the end of the platform, she could just see the guard out of the corner of her eye. She lifted the strap of her bag over her head so that her hands were now free. Green took a step towards her. The guard waved his flag and lifted his whistle to his mouth...Kate leapt. She sprang towards the train, grabbing the door handle with both hands; she flung it open and launched herself into the carriage. A startled commuter tutted and pulled the door shut as the whistle blew and the train began to move.

Green had to let her go. Dragging a high profile Scottish journalist out of a train would attract all sorts of unwanted attention. But he did have some more information so all was not lost. He headed back to the car. Evans looked expectant as he got in. “Well, did the charm work Boyo?”

“To an extent. We need to talk to the boss. We’re off to Yoost.”

“Where?”

“God knows! South Yoost. You had better get Googling again.”

~~~
~~~

Chapter 9: Wednesday in Glasgow, heading north.

Green and Evans met up with DI Parson at Glasgow airport. They had updated him by phone, intermittently as they drove back though the highlands, partly for efficiency but mainly to avoid his displeasure at their failing to capture the girl again. It was always better to give him time to calm down after bad news. He had given them a tongue lashing even after picking them up from hospital earlier in the week. The terminal complex was not large, so it was easy to spot him standing, scowling, next to the FlyBe desk. A family with several children and numerous bags were checking in. The kids were noisy and excitable, which was clearly irritating him. When one of the children accidentally ran into him it took all his self-control not to smack it and tell the parents why people like them shouldn't be allowed to travel, and should be given ASBOS just for leaving the house. The spirit of human kindness and tolerance was completely alien to him. He couldn't abide being in such public places and having to tolerate the masses.

Only a slight nod signified that he had seen his colleagues, there were no greetings or niceties. "Despite your incompetence, I have made things easy for you. Check in."

"Where are we going?"

"Benbecula. They are heading for the Outer Hebrides. That is where South Uist is. Benbecula is the nearest Airport. The flight has been delayed because of this lousy weather, I flashed my warrant card and they are letting us board. The ferry Matt Macaulay was heading for has been delayed too, so with any luck we will be there before them. All you will have to do is pick them up off the boat, you can't screw that up, can you?"

"But how are we going to get them back?" asked Green.

"Just get checked in and I'll explain it all when we get through security."

Then there was the waiting, queuing, removal of shoes and inane questions to be tolerated.

Normally Parson would have pulled rank and demanded VIP fast tracking, quoting Police Business or matters of National Security, but because that creep MacNeil was around he did not want to draw too much undue attention to himself and so was slumming it. I'll make him pay, he thought.

Following the signs for Gate Two, they seemed to be walking for ages. They passed the shops, restaurants and coffee stands, the crowds had thinned when they saw the sign for

Gates 1-3. It pointed towards a small double door on the left, which opened onto a concrete stairwell descending into a crowded waiting area.

"It's more like a bus station in Delhi than an airport lounge," muttered Green.

"Or outpatients," suggested Evans looking around. "It seems kinda familiar."

Due to the bad weather, a number of the earlier flights had been cancelled or delayed, so the place was packed with people. Practically all the seats had been taken. There were several people in wheelchairs and with plaster casts.

Being from the South of England, they found it odd that people were talking to each other. They were moaning about the weather and the delays, comparing hospital visits, catching up with relatives.

"You two will fit in well here," smirked Parson.

Looking through the window, Evans saw a small twin engine prop plane.

"God is that it! I hope this lot aren't all getting on that plane!" he shuddered.

They weren't.

A few minutes later a flight to Stornoway was called and the crowd thinned out a little. They were able to find seats in a corner away from the remaining group. A couple of people gave them curious glances. One or two nodded and wondered who they were.

Parson leaned slightly forward, indicating that he was ready to provide his briefing. He had taken a small note pad and a pencil from inside his jacket pocket. He opened the note book and began to abstractedly tap it with the pencil. He didn't really need to read the detail; the plan was already committed to memory.

"This is simple guys, not even you can mess it up. Assuming there are no more delays, our flight should get us onto the island at about fourteen hundred. The ferry they were going to catch has been cancelled. The next one is at sixteen hundred. That should give us plenty of time to be at the port to apprehend them. I have booked us into a hotel." At this point he did look at his note book, "The Mountford and we will hire a car at the airport. You can simply follow them and...," Parson shrugged his shoulders, "well, deal with them."

Green tentatively rubbed his head, "That's all very well, but he has proven a bit of a tricky character. We don't know the place, and have no resources. It not like home you know."

"I've done some digging. He is an ex Marine, but had some sort of brain injury. Couldn't get all the details, but he had neurosurgery and was on some pretty weird medication. We stick to the plan. Get what she stole from us and give her the overdose. Unfortunately killing him might not go unnoticed, but a knock on the head, causing a relapse will discredit anything he has to say in the short term. Due to your incompetence, we may have to consider a longer term solution."

"And the kid?" This was the part of the plan Green felt uneasy about.

"See what happens. You can dump him somewhere. I'm sure there are do gooder social workers on the island, just like everywhere else. Give them something to think about; a strange kid turning up out of the blue."

Evans made a face and shook his head, "Loose ends, boss."

"I know, but we have options. Look, there are only five coppers on duty on the islands at any one time. There's a local woman inspector who runs the show. Malcolm, you can chat her up. There is no CID; any experts will have to be flown in from Scotland here, Inverness I think, which is miles away, and lots of time for evidence to get contaminated. I've got the address of his family home; we won't head there unless we have to. I've arranged to have the phone bugged, just in case. We'll be able to keep track of any contact he has with his family by logging into the surveillance boy's server. I'll deal with loose ends as they happen, Rhyd."

Parson closed his notebook, there was nothing more to say. Green was staring intently at his feet. The Welshman nodded at his boss. There was an uncomfortable silence. Evans and Parson were aware that the overweight Brummy didn't really have the stomach for what they had to do, but things had gone too far to worry about that. Parson was irritated by this; Green had enjoyed the perks and should damn well clean up his own mess. Also, keeping him involved kept his mouth shut.

Finally, the flight to Benbecula was called.

They followed the aircrew out onto the apron for the short walk to the plane. All three men struggled to gather their coats and jackets around them, they weren't prepared for this. The wind seemed to cut through every tiny gap in their clothing as they waited in line to board the plane.

"And this is the improved conditions?" muttered Evans.

"Sod the weather, look at the plane. It's tiny! It's being blown about and battered by the wind even on the ground. Is this safe?" Green was feeling even more uneasy now.

"For goodness sake stop whingeing the pair of you." Snapped Parson. "Of course it's safe, just hurry up and get on board." He wanted out of the cold; his stylish mac wasn't designed for the Scottish weather. He just needed to get out of this miserable damp, alien place and go home.

It took a little while to board the plane because it was cramped inside. All thirty two seats were taken, due to the earlier flights being cancelled. Parson was seated by himself on the left of the aisle while Evans and Green were squashed together close to the front.

Neither man was prepared to admit that he was nervous, but they did exchange glances when the lights went out as the propellers started up. The noise and the vibration from the rotating blades permeated the whole aircraft rattling the nerves of the two policemen. Their sense of trepidation deepened as the pilot gave his introductory welcome. He apologised for the weather related delays, and warned that the flight may encounter "More weather". He ended with hoping "That the flight is not too uncomfortable for you."

"Shit! They don't usually say that do they, do they?" muttered Evans.

"Not on proper planes," groaned Green. Both men shifted in their seats and unconsciously tugged at their seatbelts.

The small aircraft lurched into the air as if it had been released from a catapult. The engines screamed as it climbed and turned. It was disorientating as they rose through the clouds. Neither man wanted to look out of the windows.

"It's only an hour and the girlie is going to give us a drink." Green was reassuring himself rather than the Welshman.

Green found that he had to consciously stop himself listening to the sound of the propellers as each change in pitch speed or intensity triggered another worry bead. The hostess started serving drinks, and despite disapproving sideways glances from Parson, both officers ordered large whiskies. A light flashed above the cabin door. The hostess stopped serving and consulted with the aircrew, after which she secured the trolley, returned to her seat and announced that they were expecting some turbulence.

"At least we got a drink before it gets bumpy," smiled Evans. But bumpy did not quite describe what happened next. It started to feel as if the aircraft was not so much flying but having to wade through a torrential river, being battered on all sides. Then the plane dropped... It was probably only a few feet, but it was enough to cause shrieks and grasps throughout the cabin and Evans to splash his drink all over the front of his shirt.

"Shit, shit, shit!" He swore.

The plane settled into a slightly more stable flight path when the pilot announced that they were going to "begin a descent to Benbecula", warning that it could be uncomfortable. A baby was crying and there was a palpable feeling of tension. Nobody was talking, save the few who were quietly praying. Evans couldn't help but stare out the window now as the plane hurtled towards the tiny airstrip surrounded by ocean. Green, gripping the arm rests, had his eyes shut tight and was concentrating on not being sick. Parson maintained a cool demeanour, pretending to read his newspaper, but even his nerves were rattled as the plane made its bumpy tumble to earth. He remembered some comedian making a joke about a pilot making a "controlled crash rather than landing" and that was certainly what it felt like.

The opening of the air brakes sounded painfully slow. The lowering of the landing gear juddered through the seats while the screaming of the propellers seemed to be fighting a losing battle. Finally, there were the thuds and jolts as the wheels hit the tarmac. Green didn't open his eyes or release his grip of his seat until they were finally stationary. He was as white as a sheet, and breathing deeply and slowly. Again, they had to make their way across the apron to the terminal. Green didn't notice the weather; he was relieved to be on the ground but needed to find a bathroom urgently. He felt very ill.

The other two looked around the small terminal. It comprised of one large room with check in desks at one end and a small luggage conveyor belt at the other, with seats and a tea bar in between. Large windows looked out onto the airfield. The waiting relatives and apprehensive travellers waiting to depart had obviously witnessed the dramatic landing as the place was buzzing with conversations, hugs and some tears.

It did not take long for the luggage to appear, but they were grateful for the few minutes to pull themselves together. Parson could not see a Car Hire Desk or any signs for one. Evans noticed he was looking and gave him a nudge, nodding towards a young woman holding up a sign reading, "ASK CAR HIRE".

"Let's hope she speaks English though, 'cos she wasn't a moment ago. What is it they are all saying?" he asked.

"I was hoping you'd understand it, they're speaking Gaelic. Isn't it similar to Welsh?"

"Not to me it isn't, but there are more of them talking in that than English."

"I noticed that." Agreed Parson.

To their relief, she did speak perfect English and was able to arrange a car for them. They were both surprised at the relaxed way in which there was only a cursory glance at their documentation and the lack of the endless paperwork you usually get from car hire companies. She was giving them directions to their hotel and explaining that the ferries had been delayed as well when Green reappeared from the toilets. The Lochmaddy sailing from Uig wasn't due in until six o'clock that evening, so they had time to recover and go over the plan again. They established where the local police station was and that it would take them about half an hour to travel from the hotel to the ferry port. Evans did suggest doing a trial run, but Green said that he really wasn't up to it, there were not that many roads, "What can go wrong?" he asked.

~~~
~~~

Chapter 10: Uig

It took Matt just under three hours to drive to Uig from Fort William. He knew the road well, and was not bothered by driving through the storm. Marieke had spent most of the trip staring out of the window, only this time she was not seeing the scenery. Her eyes were misty and at one point he wondered if she was crying. He tried to make the odd bit of light conversation explaining where they were going, but just got monosyllabic responses. He wondered how much Kate had explained to her.

It was only when they were driving across the Isle of Skye that it occurred to him that there might be a problem with the ferry because the storm was not abating; in fact, it was getting worse.

As they drove onto Uig Pier there were a number of cars parked forlornly waiting for a non-existent ferry. Matt drove into a nearby car park next to the Pub at the Pier. He left Marieke and Kazik in the car while he checked out the situation in the ticket office. It was still not quite daylight when he returned to the car. Marieke was changing her son's nappy on the back seat. That is a very passive child he thought; just as well really. Matt was wet and disheartened. He found it difficult to comprehend that they'd had to run again, what had he gotten himself into and more especially how was he going to get out of it? Heading home still seemed the best bet; it would put distance between them and Parson while MacNeil got things sorted out. He explained, using his phone, that they were going to have to wait until the next ferry at four o'clock. He didn't know what they would do until then, he didn't feel in the mood for doing the touristy things and didn't like waiting around. After all that had happened he couldn't help but feel exposed. He suggested that they could go for some breakfast in Portree, the nearest town, but the shops would not be open for hours. Marieke fussed over her son and fidgeted with his small bag of belongings. Leaning forward she took the phone from Matt and typed in one word. "Read!" She pointed at the printed sheets in his rucksack. He had forgotten about them. He leant over to his bag on the back seat next to Kazik who was now intent on sucking a biscuit. Nodding, he pulled out the pages and settled into the driving seat. There were six pages. He reached for the internal light switch but then changed his mind. He did not want to draw attention to themselves by putting the car lights on. He used the light on his phone to illuminate the creased pages. She was watching him intently, but she couldn't help but look away as he started to read.

He read:

"This is hard to write, it is a nightmare and some of it I do not know or cannot understand.

I will try and keep my feelings out or I will just cry for me, my friends and Kazik, and not be able to write. My name is Marieke Manover. I am twenty two years old. I come from Romania, and I lived in a small town in the Romania called Ploisti. I was a student studying to be a teacher, and my life was OK. I lived with my parents; they did not have money, so in the evenings I worked in a bar to earn a little cash.

My friend Biata worked with me. We were always being chatted up by the customers but we just laughed about it. Then one night the bar owner visited, he was from Bucharest, the capital. I was called into his office where he said that he was going to sack me because I was not "Nice enough" to the customers. I begged him not to and started to cry. He put his arms round me. At first I thought he was comforting me. Then he started touching me and pulling at my clothes. I tried to stop him. He slapped me hard and told me that if I wanted to work I had to learn to do as I was told. It is too bad to describe. He was a big smelly man, he pushed me against the door. He bit me; groped and scratched me. Hurt me. He raped me. People must have heard my cries, and seen the door shake in its frame as I was forced against it, but nobody came, they were all too scared.

When he was finished he told me to tidy myself and to go clean the toilets if I wanted to get paid. But he didn't pay me, just told me to go.

My father was furious that I had lost my job. I did not tell him about the attack, I was afraid and ashamed. I wish I had. He went to see the boss, who told him I had been sacked because I was a slut. So then, when I became pregnant my family didn't believe my story; they just thought I was a slut too. They were ashamed, I had dishonoured the family. I had to leave home and I had to leave my college course. I thought life was bad then. Biata let me stay with her and I had Kazik. It is not his fault that his father is a bastard.

Not long after that, I do not remember when, Biata came home from work to say that the boss from Bucharest was back. I was scared; I didn't like the thought of him even being in the same town as me. But this time he was looking to hire girls, for a club belonging to a friend of his in London. Biata was so excited, it was a chance for her to get out, go to London and marry Prince Harry we laughed. The Boss had told Biata to tell any friends that were interested to go and see him. Would he consider me? We talked about it for a couple of days. I was terrified of him, but I didn't want to miss the chance, so Biata and I went to see him. We should have realised, but we were too stupid. He laughed at me and agreed straight away, even with Kazik. He said he would be happy to have me and my bastard out of the country. We met his man a few days later who drove us to London in a van. I knew something was not right as soon as we got into the van but just hoped I was wrong. There were six of us squashed together in a big box. To hide from immigration, we were told. It was dark cold and scary. We could not move or straighten our legs. My body ached against the hard walls. We had water, but no food or toilet. It soon began to smell of sweat, fear and pee. Animals are treated better. I don't know how long it was. We could not see day or night. I just held my son and prayed it would get better.

Eventually, cold, stiff and hungry, we were taken to a house in London. It was old, dirty and dark. The cold and damp eat through to your bones. Biata, Kazik and I shared a small room with two mattresses on the ground and bars on the windows. Someone had painted over the glass so we could not see out. It was on the bottom floor next to the kitchen. There was a horrible smell, I didn't know what it was at first, but soon realised when I heard the gnawing at night. I was terrified they were going to bite Kazik. There were about ten girls from different countries, most spoke more English than us. That is where we met Rubin. He was a Serb, who ran the house, but he answered to the fat one, they called Malc. He was not happy about Kazik. We could hear them talking next door. He didn't think we could understand him, but we did.

He gave us what he called vitamins, to make us feel better he said. He gave them to us every day. At first they made me feel happy, so I was not worried on my first trip to the club a few days later.

I can't remember what I thought I was going to do. We were driven there at night by Rubin. He was a scrawny little man who muttered to himself. The Serb took us to the place, that day and every day. There were flashing lights loud music and a crowd. Lots of people. I was led out of the light down a dingy corridor ...smelly again. It was dark. There was a big mirror and bed. I was tied to the bed and told to wait. I think you don't need me to tell you what happened next. There were men, lots of men, again and again. Sometimes one, sometimes two or three. I can remember wondering if it was all the men in the club. Some were violent, some were just sick. It was disgusting. I hated it and myself, but I could do nothing to stop it. It was the tablets; I didn't realise at first and hated myself even more. He then took us back to the house, Malc would sometimes be there; he would take one of the girls making the other girls watch. He pulled your hair hard by the roots and laughed.

"Just to let you know who's boss," he would say. Most nights we went to the club, sometimes we were taken to parties or hotels. During the day we cried and hurt and tried to recover. Life was hell till he came back with the tablets. Several of the girls disappeared; I don't know what happened to them. One girl killed herself. I stayed alive for Kazik.

We left him in the room in the night. I was feeding him. At first I was relieved that he just slept. Then, I knew he was sleeping too much. Biata and I talked about it. It had to be the tablets. He was getting drugged through me. We decided we had to stop this; we had to escape, before he or us died. We would stop taking the medicine, because it stopped you thinking, then we would plan an escape. We worked out how we could pretend to swallow the tablets and then get rid of them.

Biata listened to them talking in the kitchen. They were making a plan to sell Kazik. It was even more important that we left. She found out that there was a bus station nearby. She heard Malc telling someone how to get there. It was a start.

But there was a bad side to not taking the tablets. Kazik started to cry. He was cold, scared and hungry. The other girls tried to help with him, but the man with Malc, the little ratty one, kept threatening to "Shut him up properly."

The other bad thing was that we started to feel all of what was happening to us. The bruising, tearing flesh, being mauled about like meat over and over again. The dirt and slime of sweat, semen and sick in every hole in your body. Being slapped, slashed and punched night after night with no escape from the torture.

Biata had another problem. Big nose, the tall skinny one used to turn up sometimes, with Malc. He looked and sounded like a reptile, sneering at us through his slanty eyes. He didn't speak, just hissed his evil commands. You could tell that Malc was scared of him too. He "liked" Biata, he would take her to another room and do things. She would never say what, but afterwards she would just shake her head, cry and bleed. When he came that night she hadn't taken the tablets, and she couldn't pretend.

I did not know if big nose knew that Kazik was still there. I think they were too scared to tell him that they hadn't got rid of him yet. I held my child tight and hid under the blanket as soon as we heard his voice. The door knob rattled as he unlocked the door. He flicked a switch and the cold harsh light flooded the room. I hate myself that I lay still as if dead while he dragged Biata away...but I do not think I could have done anything.

All we could hear was her screaming, and screaming and screaming. Then she stopped. I knew she was dead. The noise must have raised the alarm as people started banging on the door and there was a lot of shouting. People started to run around. I peered through a corner of my cover and realised that Big Nose had not closed the room door: It was open! I thought it might be my chance. I heard doors bang and footsteps up and down the stairs. There was talking, a woman giving orders, but they were all upstairs. I took my chance, grabbing Kazik and our small bag of things; I slowly eased the door open. There was nobody there, but I could hear the woman and Big Nose arguing above me. I headed quickly for the front door. I could not open it, it was too stiff. Suddenly there was the sound of footsteps again. They were coming back down the stairs. In the wall there was another door. I opened it; it was a large cupboard with some sort of cleaning stuff in it and old clothes. I climbed in and we curled up small behind the coats. Because of my bag the door would not close properly, I was scared that they would notice me. The woman stood just by the door; she was talking about, "My Report," or something. Big Nose was saying, "Give it to me." She said "No," and sounded very angry with him. She went to open the door; she struggled too, but it moved for her.

I am not sure how the next part happened. Looking through the small gap in the door, first

I saw the woman walking down the steps out of the house. Then Malc rushed forward and tried to grab her bag. They struggled, she fell backwards banging her head on the ground. She did not get up. Big Nose went forward. He did not help her, just grabbed the bag and threw it back into the house. After that he started shouting again. They got the car and carried her into it then drove away. Only the Serb was left. Big Nose had told him to do something, I do not know what, but he went back upstairs to where Biata was. Kazik and I were alone again. I could see the bag across the hall. It was my last chance. I quietly crept out of the cupboard. Kazik whimpered but he was too scared to make much noise. I grabbed the woman's bag and gave the door a hard pull. I knew if she could do it, so could I. It didn't move at first, but I knew my life depended on it, because if they caught me, I would be dead too. Finally it swung open. I remembered the bus station and ran until I saw it. I panicked first, thinking that I had no money, then I checked the woman's bag; there was a purse with paper money. I did not know which bus to get on. I saw one that had the words "six hours" on the side, so I thought it would be going far away. It was number 7. I decided to buy the ticket for that one. I looked round when I was buying the ticket thinking that they would be coming after me any minute. People gave me nasty looks and shook their heads. I thought I would never get away. But finally I did. I did not know where I was going, but I thought I had escaped. We sat at the back of the bus away from everyone. I looked through the bag. As well as her purse, there was a plastic container with a note book, small bottles of fluid and a black square thing that looked like a computer device. I looked at the book. I didn't understand all the writing, but I saw the words "East European" and the date. So I thought it was about Biata, and that it was what Big Nose wanted. I have kept it.

The bus drove a long way. I did not know if there would be borders or police but there were none. When we finally stopped I was able to use the rest of her money to buy us some food. I had been walking around the city looking for somewhere to sleep for the night when they found me again and I met you."

Matt was stunned. He didn't know what to say. Instinctively he leant over and squeezed her hand, not trusting himself to speak. Holding her hand tightly, he could feel himself breathing slowly and deeply. He pursed his lips and shook his head. He couldn't believe that such terrible things had happened to the slight girl sitting next to him. She had been quiet while he read. Kazik had fallen asleep on her lap. As she turned and looked at him he saw a single tear roll down her cheek. He picked up his phone, there was so much he wanted to say, he didn't know where to start. He typed: "They will not get away with it. We will get them. I will help you. I promise."

Reading this, Marieke gave him one of her weak smiles and shrugged. She spoke slowly in English, almost whispering. "They are very bad men.... Dangerous."

Matt agreed with this. Up until this point he had thought that they were simply dealing with bent Sassenach Poileas, who just needed to be sent back home with their legs slapped. Now he realised just how dangerous and desperate they were.

It was now daylight. Matt needed to move.

“Come on,” he said, starting the car. “We’re not sitting here waiting for trouble. Let’s get some breakfast and work out a plan. I think best with a cup of tea.” Marieke didn’t really understand what he had said, but she appreciated the positive tone.

Matt's mind was racing as he drove back to Portree, hoping to find an open coffee shop. Even if only part of the story were true, it was still horrific. Having spent the last day with her and the child he could see no reason why she should lie. You wouldn't be making stories up about the police to get a visa he reasoned.

Deciding to believe the story had consequences though. It meant that there were three men, killers, who were chasing them with a vested interest in silencing Marieke. Kate was taking a copy of the statement to MacNeil in Glasgow, but they had to really disappear until they knew it was safe for her to give her evidence. They couldn't go to his mum’s. He couldn't endanger her or Iona. He didn't want to leave any trail of them being in Uist. In fact, he didn't even want any record of them being on the boat.

By the time they were sitting in the back of a crowded cafe ordering breakfast rolls he was ready to explain his plan. He had climbed, walked and camped all over the Uists since he was a small boy. He had sometimes thought that he knew parts of the coastline that most people didn't know really existed. What hope would a bunch of low life Londoners have of finding them? All he had to do was talk her into it.

Marieke sat pushing her food around her plate. She didn't even attempt to feed her son. “It’s good,” encouraged Matt, licking his lips and patting his belly. Kazik laughed, but she just shrugged listlessly. He offered the boy a piece of sausage, which he took, imitating Matt's gestures, then began to suck. This raised a smile on his mother's face, but not much more.

“It’s ok. I have an idea.” He typed into his phone. He said the words as he showed her the screen. She raised an eyebrow as she looked at it. It didn’t look hopeful. He, however, knew they had no choice, so, slowly, by using the phone, hand gestures, and drawings on napkins, he explained to her what he had in mind. At first she said nothing, she shrugged and shook her head. Slowly she started to say things then stopped in frustration. Gradually she started to ask questions. After considering his answers, she began to make suggestions as to things they would need. They were thinking along the same lines. They had a plan.

~~~
~~~

Chapter 11: Disappearing

At least the wind has dropped, Matt thought as he walked up the gangway boarding the ferry. He was wearing a blue beanie hat that covered his stubbly ginger hair and carried a rucksack with a built-in child carrier. Sitting in the carrier was a toddler in a bright pink romper suit. He had explained to Marieke that Parson's men would be asking about a couple with a small boy. They had scoured through the charity shops in Portree to find the things to make them look different. What would be seen was a man with a little girl. Just to the left as he boarded the ship was a small windowless lounge reserved for lorry drivers, which was rarely used, and despite the sign on the door, seldom locked. He tried the handle and smiled as the door slid to the left. It was a small dull room with a bench seat and a table. He could see why it was not often used, unless you wanted sleep or solitude. He put his rucksack with Kazik down on the floor.

"Shhh," he whispered to the child. "I'll be back in a sec." Stepping out of the room, he slid the door shut again as he waited for Marieke to follow in the crowd.

She was dressed as a hiker too, in khaki walking trousers, boots and a waterproof jacket. She had the hood up and a grey scarf covering her face. A thick fleece under her jacket filled her out. and completely changed her appearance. The nappy bag had been stuffed into a back pack. She walked with a determined stride looking down and avoiding eye contact with fellow passengers and Calmac staff. She didn't look at the seaman in a high-vis jacket as she handed him her boarding card in the name of Miss M. MacDonald. She turned left and kept walking as Matt had told her. As if from nowhere, Matt appeared in front of her. Without a word, he took her arm and pulled her into the small room, sliding the door closed behind them. He turned the lock. It was crazy, thought Matt, to simply consider boarding the ferry as an achievement, but they had done it.

The crossing took just under two hours. Matt kept a note of the time in order to plan their next move. Once he was fairly sure that they were not going to be disturbed he asked Marieke if he could look at what she had taken from the woman's hand bag. He had not wanted to do so in public as he was simply not sure what he would find. She had to stand up to open and rummage through her big bag. She pulled a jumper and some food out, and finally the battered nappy bag. She placed it on the table, took out a couple of the baby things that they had bought in Fort William, then handed him a fawn coloured leather bag. It was a cross between a satchel and a hand bag, with buckles and fastenings to be negotiated before you reached a zipped compartment. Definitely security conscious, thought Matt as he worked his way through all the fastenings.

As Marieke watched and Kazik crawled around on the floor, he placed the contents on the table. There was an orange rectangular purse, reporter's notebook, lip balm, a couple of pens and a sealed plastic bag with a couple of vials containing a congealed, foul coloured gunk. There were some tissues and a couple of receipts that showed the owner had done some latenight shopping on the night of the third of April, the Saturday before he had met Marieke in Glasgow. No mobile phone. He wondered where it and the shopping were. She must have left a car somewhere. He wished he had gloves, he handled everything tentatively. Opening the purse, he took out the driving licence. There was a photo of a woman in her mid thirties with brown curly hair and intelligent eyes. The name read Rebecca Wilson. She lived somewhere in North London. He showed the photo to Marieke. "Her?" he asked. She nodded sadly. I do hope she's still alive, he thought. There was what looked like a work identification card in the same name, with a similar photograph. It identified her as an employee of the Metropolitan Police, a forensic technician.

He started leafing through the note book. It was very methodical, with most items dated and some titled. Some entries were recording meetings or events with the participants listed. The last page had the same date as the receipt. He had difficulty making it out as the writing was more scribbled than on other pages. She must have been agitated or in a hurry, he thought.

He read out loud:

- *03/04/2014 – Off duty*

- *Emergency call. Woodhurst road. Commotion and screaming.*

-Possible brothel

- *Young Eastern European girl, recently dead.*

-Signs of Sexual trauma

-Took blood and fluid samples

-3 Police already on the scene...Evans; Green; ??

-Don't know how they got there so soon.

-Crime scene compromised

-Uncooperative.

-Threatened.

Matt couldn't stop his hand shaking. Was this girl dead too? Just out doing her shopping then walking into hell. The third name had to be Parson. This would verify Marieke's statement. He was not convinced what could be gleaned from the toxic looking samples, but you never knew. They had to get this to Glasgow. It was the evidence that would put Parson behind bars.

He replaced everything carefully into the bag. They secured them into the nappy bag, then back into the rucksack.

Matt looked at his watch. It was time to be moving again.

They were about fifteen minutes away from Lochmaddy. In about ten minutes they would be inviting drivers to re-join their cars, however, they often opened the door to the car deck early when the ship was busy to allow access for crew preparing for docking. He hoped this was the case for today. Telling Marieke to wait for him and ensuring that he could not hear voices in the corridor, he eased the door open. There were a couple of people about, but they paid him little attention. It only took him a minute to confirm that access to the car deck was open. Collecting the girl and child, he walked quickly towards the car deck stairs and slipped down without being noticed. It was noisy and smelly as they made their way through the tightly packed vehicles. They struggled with the big rucksack on. Marieke understood Matt's plan, but she was not convinced it was going to work as he moved from car to car. Suddenly he stopped, turned to her and smiled. He pointed towards a small coach.

"C'mon," he grinned, "this is our lift." They moved quickly toward the bus. It had a flag draped across the windows saying "Iochdar Saints... Champions!!" and as he expected, the passenger door was not locked and they were able to climb in and find a space at the back on the floor amongst the bags and kit. "Soccer Team?" Marieke asked.

"Football." he replied. "The best football team!"

There wasn't much room; they had no choice but to cuddle up closely together. She leant back against Matt's chest as he wrapped his arms around her. There was no tension, it felt natural; a moment of peace for both of them. She felt warm and reassured in the dark; safe in his arms, but she knew it was a feeling that couldn't last.

~~~
~~~

Chapter 12: Lochmaddy

At the Mountford Hotel in Benbecula, the three policemen were recovering from their flight. The hotel, the main one in the islands, was a centre for local community activity. It was a popular evening meeting place and despite being frequently slated on Trip Advisor served good food and beer. It was popular with tourist coach trips and locals. It was the only bar open during the week in the area. The rooms were small and the decor was of an era of its own. It was not the most modern of hotels. Parson felt he was in a time warp, but he was told that it was the hotel that visiting business men used, so he hoped that they would blend in. On arrival, he couldn't imagine why any business man would want to visit such an out of the way place, or mingle with the coach loads of SAGA visitors. His PA had told him that there were more exclusive hotels on the North and South Islands, but he couldn't bear the thought of being seen anywhere respectable with Green and Evans. B&Bs would have been cheaper, but their movements could well have been noticed by an inquisitive host. He had to book the rooms quickly; he wanted things as unobtrusive and easy as possible.

He joined his colleagues in the bar where they were drinking tea and poring over a map that they had borrowed from the unmanned reception desk, trying to pronounce the local place names and laughing at each other's attempts.

"For God sake, you two, shut up! You'll get us thrown out! Have you worked out how to get to the port?" He asked, looking at the map.

"Yes, the barman's given us directions. It's one straight road and signposted, with big pictures of boats just in case we can't read the signs."

"Which is just as well really, have you seen some of these place names?" observed Green. Parson ignored him. "D'you know how long it'll take?"

"About half an hour he says," replied Evans nodding towards the barman. "We'll give it forty minutes or so."

His boss sat down at the table. "And are we clear about what we have to do this time?" He looked at his men, from one to the other as if they were truculent children.

"Arrest them and get them into the car if they are on foot and it's feasible, or simply follow them and report back, to deal with them tomorrow. Evans imitated speech marks when he said "Arrest them". Green picked up on the thought. He was leaning forward now and shifting his weight in his seat.

"Should we try and enlist help from the local cops?"

“There are only five of them. Top dog is a local woman called Florence Macrury, I can’t see how she would help.”

“It’s just that he’s, well, you know, handy. You haven’t seen him.”

Parson dismissed this. “His medical record says he is not fit to tie his shoe laces. Tap him on the back of the head and he’ll crumble. There’s two of you for God’s sake; use your brains!”

Green didn’t seem convinced, but Evans was more confident. “Look you, he took us by surprise last time, that’s all.” He adjusted the sun glasses he had bought to hide his bruised face. “I’ve got a score to settle anyway.”

“What time are you leaving then?” Parson, in his usual style had closed the conversation.

“Time to get on with things.”

The bar man had said it would be easy, just turn left at the T junction, then follow the ferry signs. So, neither man was worried. They passed a garage on the left and headed north. Very soon the road became single track with passing places. They had noticed these whilst driving from the airport, but Evans was driving too fast and several times found himself having to stop suddenly and at one point had to reverse back to a passing place to allow a lorry to pass.“This is ridiculous.” He muttered, as Green laughed at him when he had to slow down yet again.

They drove towards North Uist. Evans wasn’t sure what to expect. He hadn’t quite realised that he would be driving over a causeway onto a separate island. He just thought it was a separate borough or place like East Finchley is just a part of London. The islands from Berneray, through North and South Uist, Benbecula and down to Eriskay are linked by a series of bridges and causeways, so it is possible to drive from one island to another. The system is understood by locals, but could be disorientating and distracting if you were not paying attention to where you were. Just after the causeway the road widened to allow two-way traffic again. Frustrated, Evans put his foot down to make up time. But as they rounded the corner he was confronted by another obstacle.

“Sheep!” yelled Green as the car careered to a halt.

“I can see that,” muttered Evans, “but what the hell are they doing here?”

The road was blocked by a flock of about eight sheep just meandering in front of them. He leaned heavily on his horn to scare them, but only succeeded in making them run a bit, but not actually moving out of the way. He edged forward and managed to pass them, but both men were beginning to feel rattled by what they considered to be an increasingly hostile environment. All the road signs were in Gaelic with the English translation in smaller letters underneath. They found this hard to understand as even the English translations were unfamiliar and hard to pronounce. They soon stopped reading them and were just following the ferry symbols on the sign posts, which is why when they reached an electronic sign showing a boat near Lochmaddy they turned left, not realising that there might be more than one port.

The road narrowed and became twisty. They turned right, then right again. "I thought he said it was a straight road?" commented Green." I saw the Lochmaddy sign, we should be there by now." They had to drive on a bit before they could find a place to stop, consult the map and realise they were on the wrong road. By the time they turned around and headed back onto the main road, they were met by a constant flow of traffic. It was as they got to the port that they realised it was actually people leaving the ferry. Evans and Green had missed the boat! It had already arrived and most of the passengers had already disembarked and were on their way.

"Shit; Shit; Shit!" muttered Green as they pulled into an empty car park.

"This is becoming a habit," thought Evans. About two hundred metres away he saw a Police car. Standing next to it was a woman officer and a port official. He got out of the car and walked towards them, pulling his warrant card from his jacket as he approached.

"Here we go," muttered Evans as he got out of the car to follow him.

Green introduced himself and explained that they were Metropolitan Police Officers tracking down a wanted felon and her accomplice, who they believed had been travelling on the ferry that had just docked. That they had planned to meet the ferry, but been delayed by road incidents. He mentioned that he wanted to speak with the police woman separately about livestock on the roads.

The Calmac employee suggested that they go through to the office to look at the boarding cards and ask the crew if they had seen anyone matching the description of the fugitives. The Police woman followed. Green didn't notice that she was simmering, annoyed at his sudden appearance. She did not introduce herself or make any comment. She was making a note of the name and planning to investigate why this man hadn't followed normal procedures and who did he think he was that he could address her as if she was some junior skivvy.

The discussion in the office was of no help. They didn't expect them to be travelling under their own names, but there were no boarding cards for a family group of the right age with a small child. The crew didn't remember seeing them, and when it was mentioned that it was Matt Macaulay that they were looking for, several crew members were adamant that they knew him and he was definitely not on the boat.

They drove back slowly to their hotel, disheartened, apprehensive and fed up. Had the sister contacted him and warned him? Or had she been lying to send them on a wild goose chase in the first place? Could they have disembarked without being seen? What neither man mentioned, but both quietly dreaded was Parson's reaction to them losing their quarry again. It didn't bear thinking about.

By unspoken agreement they played down their travel difficulties when explaining what happened to their boss. He listened without comment. His eyes narrowing when he heard that they had spoken with the local police. They were seated in a corner of the bar. He had been working and had his lap top and some paperwork in front of him. He started fiddling with a pencil, then, bent apart a paperclip that had been holding some documents together. Not good signs.

"Should we give his family a call?" ventured Evans

"No, the locals will do that now, but it might be worth you chatting the Macrury woman up to get background and minimise any damage you have done. Last thing we want is her whingeing back to Glasgow about us being here." He nodded at Green.

They agreed to meet later for dinner. The two junior officers set off again to try and find the Policewoman, but to no avail. They drove to the Police Station in Balivanich. The constable there could not tell them where she was or when she would be back. He suggested they left their contact details and how long they planned to be on the island so that she could get back to them. In fact, he was following specific instructions not to tell them anything and to get as much information from them as possible. They drove around the few streets trying to spot a squad car, but it was nowhere to be seen. They were not keen on venturing out into open country after their previous experience so after a decent interval headed back to the hotel.

Dinner started as a cold silent affair. Parson didn't do small talk at the best of times, and now was not the best of times. Evans was allegedly intent on something on his I phone, while Green stared across the room.

They were halfway through their meal when the bar suddenly became very crowded. There was an influx of young lads obviously celebrating some sort of football match. They were in various groups, and were voicing a particularly tuneless rendition of "Oh when the Saints... come marching in..." and cheering.

"This is all we need," moaned Parson.

"I'll get us another drink." Green stood, putting his cutlery down. He wasn't feeling generous, but wanted the opportunity to talk with somebody ... anybody; light hearted banter was just what he needed. There was a group of lads standing at the bar laughing and joking.

He was disappointed however as he got closer and realised that they were speaking Gaelic so he was unable to understand or join in. He gave the barman a smile and was about to order a drink when he heard one of the crowd mention Matt Macaulay. The youth said something and they all laughed. Somebody else made a comment referring to Matt again, obviously to everyone's amusement.

"Same again pal?" offered the barman.

"Sure, errrm, can I buy these guys a drink too? To celebrate?" His offer was passed on, and a couple of the group turned around to see who it was from. One, a bit the worse for wear, spoke up.

"Thanks *math tha*, You a Saints fan too?" He wobbled as he turned and had to hold the bar to balance himself. His glistening eyes showed the extent of the day's celebrations.

"Not as such, but I do like to see local teams do well. I'm just here trying to track down distant relatives. So, what did the Saints win?" They talked for a minute or two about football and Green discovered the young man was known as DJ. Green finally introduced what he really wanted to talk about.

"I heard one of you guys mention Matt Macaulay. I think he may be a second or third cousin of mine. Is he about?"

"No, that's the joke. He came back on the ferry today, but Tiny's saying he's picked up a bird, but he's too scared to take her home to his Mam. They hitched a lift in the team mini bus and have talked Callum into taking them to the east side. Camping in this weather!" He laughed, slurring his words and slurping at his drink.

"Wow," chuckled Green. He wasn't acting, he felt distinctly light hearted.

"Whereabouts?"

"They were talking about Charlie's Cave...not sure it exists myself." DJ replied. Green tried to get more details, but his luck ran out. Despite the amount of alcohol consumed, DJ's defences were up. He felt he had said too much already and didn't like the further questions. Whilst he would have happily shared the details with his neighbours, he had said enough to this stranger. Instead he changed the subject and put Green to the test. Pointing to a well-built man who had just walked in, he told Green:

"That's Sketch Macaulay. He runs the local Taxi and is a second cousin of Matt's too. You must be related to him as well?"

"I'll have to catch up with him," smiled Green. The man was laughing and joking over the other side of the bar with the football fans, but didn't look like the type to be messed with.

Also, he didn't want to be talking with a relative just in case Matt had confided in him. Still, it was useful to know.

He paid for the drinks and was happy with his investment as he re-joined his colleagues.

DJ felt uneasy about the conversation; he watched Green return to his table, and decided that he would have a word with Sketch about this so called distant relative.

Very soon the three policemen had fired up the lap top, and with their map were trying to find Charlie's Cave and work out how to get there. Parson was very nearly cheerful. The fugitives and their evidence were back within their grasp once again... in an environment that it would be very easy for them to have an accident in.

~~~
~~~

Chapter 13: A Walk in the Hills.

The thing about living in South Uist is that everyone knows, or at least think they know, all about you. People generally knew that Matt Macaulay had been in the services, some sort of hero. Then that he had been ill, and a bit odd; had a big operation and was on the mend. The fact that the English police were chasing him was a source of great local interest, especially as one had claimed to be a distant relative. And news had spread quickly.

The three visitors were, however, oblivious to all of this as they came down to breakfast the following morning. They had been up late scouring references to "Charlie's Cave," and how to get there. As DJ had indicated the previous night, there was some doubt as to whether it actually existed or was just the stuff of legend. The Ordnance Survey map and website indicated that on the east coast of Glen Corrodale was a secluded valley with abandoned croft dwellings situated at its foot on Corrodale Bay. It was claimed that there was a cave lying at the top of a steep slope, in a rock face, where Bonnie Prince Charlie had hidden from the English Redcoats during the Jacobite Rebellion in 1745. It was said to be about twenty metres from the remains of a cottage that can be used as a land mark to identify it. Evans was reading all this from his notebook.

"What we don't know is how he got there. There isn't a road as such, but there are paths, perhaps on a bike, or by boat to the bay, like the prince himself."

"How romantic," sneered Parson. "But that is definitely the place?"

"Looks like it. One web site refers to it as an eight hour return walk for tourists. The girl on reception says visitors do it all the time!"

Green snorted at this, but Parson looked thoughtfully at his watch. It was only 07.30 in the morning.

"It would give us the element of surprise though."

"An eight hour walk?" Green looked open mouthed, questioningly at both his colleagues. "And what we gonna do when we get there? Not as if they're going to walk back with us? I ain't carrying the kid!"

Parson breathed deeply and rolled his eyes. Not having a pencil to fidget with he picked up a teaspoon and held it between his thumbs and started to twist it abstractedly.

"The way I see it, we deal with the girl as we always planned, grab the bag and give her the dope. The kid ..." He hesitated, as he was thinking on his feet now.

“We were going to leave it to be found, but that might have to change now.” He didn’t want to be more explicit.

“As for Macaulay, well that will have to look like an accident. People know he’s there so they’ll go find him when he doesn’t show in a couple of days. They might even pick the brat up then,” he nodded to Green. “Anyway, we make a big show of giving up looking this evening; ask the woman plod to keep searching for them. Then when they find the bodies, we say we were right all along and blame Glasgow for letting them go.”

He wasn’t looking forward to the walk himself, but really didn’t trust the other two not to screw up again. He felt pleased with himself at the neatness of his solution and he thought that he might even enjoy its execution.

Evans was still leafing through a pile of tourist maps and brochures. He looked up. “It says here that you drive to a place called Loch Eynort and follow the path from there, that will cut some of the time down too. We have to get as far as a place called Crosgard, which is a pass, it gets a bit rocky but then there is a flat bit, but after that there is what looks like a path to follow. Even you can do that Malc.” His boss smiled coldly while Green just humphed.

Parson was focussed now. “What are we waiting for then?” With a burst of energy and uncharacteristic cheerfulness he chivvied the other two to get themselves ready and into the car. He waited in the car when Evans insisted that they stopped at a local shop to pick up supplies. Finally, they drove southwards to Loch Eynort and parked up. They left the car at the road’s end fully expecting to put an end to their problems permanently that day.

The sun was shining hazily, it was warm with just a light breeze as they set off. The storms of the previous day had blown themselves out, leaving the islands and hundreds of small lochans, glittering in the morning sun. They didn’t actually check the weather forecast, but commented, with a hint of irony, that it was a good day for a walk. It might have been, had they been sticking to a path.

The beginning of the trail had been restored by a local conservation project and meandered pleasantly through the hills. Over the first hour they felt they were making good time and that the day would be less arduous than first considered. Evans didn’t quite share the optimism. He was map reading, so understood the terrain ahead, and was a little worried about his colleagues’ lack of preparation. He had walked in the Welsh hills as a young man, so remembered some of the guidance given.

“Remember guys, avoid the green grass,” he called. Green just stared uncomprehendingly, thinking he was being insulted in some way, so the Welsh man had to explain about spotting and avoiding bogs. It was obviously news to his fellow walkers. He and Parson had both managed to dig out trainers, which would have to do in the absence of walking boots; they didn't want to buy any, as that might have drawn attention to their trip. Green unfortunately had only brought one pair of shoes, so was walking in his usual brogues. All three men wore jeans. Parson was carrying his city mac and a small bag, but Green did not have a coat at all. Evans had a small rucksack with some sandwiches and a couple of bottles of water, a small compass, a map and his phone. But that was all of their kit.

"We'll be fine if all goes well," he thought but his misgivings increased as he became more aware that the other two really didn't understand the enormity of what they had undertaken.

Heather slopes surrounded them and the path wound up through the landscape disappearing round the shoulder of a hill in front of them. They had to travel north east, crossing over the pass to follow a stream into Glen Liadail and Evans told them to look out for a ruined cottage as a landmark. The path was becoming increasingly difficult underfoot. He warned the others that it would be running out soon and then they would be heading across country. They were to walk up to the brow of the hill, and then to turn right to head down towards the cottage. But the route was plagued with false summits which really began to bug Malcolm Green. He was beginning to tire and became despondent as several times he reached what he thought was the top of the ascent, only to see a further ridge on the horizon beyond. He sounds like a kid asking are we there yet every ten minutes, thought Evans.

After another half a mile, the path finally disappeared into the gorse and heather. They could still see the line of the trail and where it emerged further down the hill, but it would mean a scramble across the hill side. Leading the way, Evans paused and opened a bottle of water as the other two caught up.

"You sure you are up for this, lads?"

"What choice do we have? It's only a short stretch, just got to watch how we go." Parson was trying to sound more positive than he felt. He wasn't prepared to admit that he hadn't really thought this through, but he was desperate to get the whole situation resolved. So, despite it being against his better judgement, he knew they had to go on. He hoped that Green's resolve was as strong.

They started into the heather. Almost immediately Evans knew it was a mistake. The heather was bouncy and soft on the top, but it gave them no clue to the rocky terrain beneath it and it hid the brambles that tore at their legs and ankles. Parson lost his footing, and stumbled, ripping his expensive coat on the brambles. Green had resorted to inching his way down the hill on his backside. This was a safer option, but it really slowed him down and more alarmingly he was heading off in the wrong direction.

"Malc!" called Evans, pointing him back to the track. He was becoming more and more convinced that they were heading for disaster.

Once recovered from his fall Parson seemed to find a second wind and renewed determination. He managed to develop a gangling stride that allowed him to at least pick up a little speed and direction. He was finally managing to keep up despite the difficult terrain. Evans pointed ahead.

"Just a short scramble over those rocks then we are back on the path again." The hill seemed to be sporadically littered with large boulders of odd shapes and sizes that really slowed them down. "We'll need to keep to the right though," he added. The comment was superfluous really. The rock face was not steep and would only be about a ten minute clamber but to the left they could both see the two hundred foot drop that lurked about three feet away. "We're going to have to talk Malc over that," he sighed. Parson nodded resignedly.

Green was making a meal out of crossing the heather. The mountainside really was a foreign, hostile, environment to him. He was travelling slowly, on all fours, leaning back, crab style. He assessed each move before he made it, often taking the long way around every rock or bush. The other two were waiting at the foot of the rocks. Parson was becoming impatient. This was wasting time, time they didn't have. Evans was trying to call encouragement and direction, Parson kept interjecting with insults and threats. Malcolm Green was feeling very stressed. Because of their vantage point Evans and Parson had a better view of the trail and could see what they thought would be an easier route for him and Evans managed to convince him to stand up and walk towards them. He was still very tentative, but seemed to gain confidence as there was only a short distance to go. Parson was still haranguing him to hurry up, so he started a shambling run.

The map had shown a number of burns or streams that flowed across the hill side. As small blue lines on paper they looked innocuous, none of them realised how the stream that was trickling down the hillside in front of Green had eroded the peat to make it a deep sharp gully. Had he not been running he may well have stepped over it. Unfortunately, he didn't. Icy water rushed into his shoe, and as he stepped forward, up to his knees. The shock of this caused him to try and jump out, but he lost his footing on a slippery rock and tumbled head first into the burn, twisting his ankle on the way. Cold, wet and in pain he lay in the undergrowth moaning.

There was no sympathy from his boss. Evans managed to calm him down and tried to convince him that his ankle wasn't broken. He helped Green to the relative safety of the rock face, but it was obvious that he did not want to go any further. They had no pain killers or any sort of first aid kit. Evans wanted to call for help but Parson wouldn't even consider it. He did think of just going on and leaving him there, it would be quicker and he wouldn't have to put up with the moaning but he knew that would lead to consequences that he could not control...he didn't trust Green; the man was too weak.

Evans tried the practical approach, reminding them all that it was nearly midday, they had been walking nearly three hours already, so must be over half way; it would be easier now, just downhill to the bay. Soon. He wasn't basing this advice on any real knowledge, but Green seemed to be listening to it. He also argued that it would take hours for the rescue services to reach them this high up. The map showed some sort of shelter closer to the ruin. If needs be, they could leave him there. He argued that they would be better moving to somewhere more accessible. Green could see the logic in this, and finally agreed to soldier on.

The scramble over the rocks wasn't as bad for Green as his colleagues had anticipated. He was able to crawl for most of it, which meant that he could avoid putting weight on his sprained ankle, the relief of which outweighed his concerns about the nearby drop. As they scrambled over the top they were all pleased to see a relatively flat plain in front of them. Perhaps the Welshman was right and it would be easier from now on they thought, as Evans studied the map to confirm the direction in which they should be heading. It was difficult with the absence of distinguishable land marks.

"Just head north east," he decided.

They looked for something to serve as a walking stick for Green, but there were no bushes or trees about at all, the harsh Hebridean climate being hostile to trees and bushes, especially in such an exposed location. Whether it was due to the relentless salt laden wind, sheep or deer, Evans didn't care, he felt that even the environment was conspiring against him as he hobbled behind the other two. Parson took the lead, striding forward, believing that they were nearly there and with a little more effort this nightmare would be over. It started to get noticeably wet underfoot but he didn't let that deter him.

"You sure this is the right direction?" he called behind him. He was getting frustrated, they had been walking for about ten minutes yet everything still looked the same. The terrain made it difficult to see the forward route. He couldn't hear Evans' reply, so turned to face him, walking backwards so as not to slow down too much. He was alright for two or three steps, then something made him turn around...A noise, or perhaps just sixth sense, but it gave him just enough time to see the muddy bog he was falling into. He yelled as he landed on his backside in the peaty mud. His long arms and legs were splayed at unnatural angles. Swearing profusely, he tried to regain his balance and dignity. Keen to keep his travel bag out of the dirty water, he threw it onto a nearby boulder that looked as if it might be drier. Evans walked to help him, but even from this distance away Parson could hear Green's belly laugh. He was obviously enjoying the reversal of fortune. Parson put his hand out to push himself up but became concerned as he realised the ground would not take his weight; any pressure on the mud made him sink in further. He could feel the boggy dampness rising on his hips where he sat.

"Quick man - I'm sinking!" he shouted at his colleague. His attempts to right himself were only making matters worse. Evans edged to the side of the bog, trying to find secure footing. He was a lot smaller than his boss and didn't want to be pulled in. He called to Green to hurry up and help. They tried taking hold of their boss's hands to pull him out, but they were too wet and slippery. They had to lean forward and grab handfuls of his jumper each in order to get some purchase, all hoping that the material would hold. It did, but one shoe and his coat were sacrificed in the attempt to save him. Once on firmer ground, he shook off any assistance and staggered over to the nearby boulders and sat down. He was cold and wet and badly shaken, covered in mud up to his waist and the hilltop wind cut right through him.

"We gonna call for help now?" asked Green. Still smarting from the lack of sympathy he had received. His boss didn't answer him.

"Don't tell me; you're going to hop and will dry off in no time." He sneered.

"Shut the fuck up,"....was the hissed reply. "Give me time to think!"

"Rhyd, can you find my shoe?"

Evans was surprised at the request, not quite sure where he was expected to start.

"What do you mean? It's in the mud, isn't it? You won't get it back from there." He avoided making eye contact with his boss because he had a horrible feeling that he knew exactly what his boss wanted was for him to venture into the mud.

"Just try will you. I won't get far without it and we can't sit up here all day."

Evans knew that tone. You could argue with him for hours when he was in a mood like this, and still end up doing what he wanted. The only change would be that he would be in a worse mood than normal. He was also not sure of the alternatives if he couldn't find the shoe. He walked back over to the edge of the bog. He reckoned it was about a meter wide, but there was no real way of telling. Rubbing his chin, he thought for a moment then proceeded to take his jacket, jumper and shirt off and fold them in a neat little pile beside him. He took the compass from around his neck and the map from his back pocket and placed them on top of his clothes. He couldn't quite believe what he was about to do, but just felt he was better getting on with it. Testing the terrain with his feet, he found a suitable spot to lie down and shimmied himself as close as he could to the muddy hole. Cursing under his breath he plunged his right arm into the muddy ground.

"Yuk, gross!" laughed Green.

"Thanks for your encouragement pal...I need some help here."

"I ain't doing that...I'm not going in there!"

"No, I need a stick or something to reach further. I'm not going to get very far like this."

Still hobbling, Green scouted round and managed to find part of a discarded fence post with some wire tangled around it. It was about three feet long.

"That might do, bring it here," agreed Evans who was still half lying on the ground but with his arm extracted from the mud. Green joined him, kneeling down beside the little pile of clothes, close to his colleague. He passed him the fence post then sat back. He didn't notice knocking the compass and map onto the ground behind him. He offered advice and tried to direct the search, but it soon became apparent that they had no chance of finding the shoe.

"Sorry boss, it ain't comin' out!" the Welshman called. Parson was still sitting on the boulder, but had turned away from them to shield himself from the wind that had started to blow more strongly.

"Watch out Malc, you're making my stuff muddy..." Green stood up quickly trying to avoid the Welshman's clothes. Stumbling due to his sore ankle he had to step backwards to steady himself. He didn't hear the crunch of the compass cracking under his foot.

Parson didn't speak as Evans redressed, he was staring into space, deep in thought.

"Pass the map and compass then." Green looked around him.

"They were just there, on my jumper." Evans walked over to where Green was standing and crouched down. "You idiot," he cried as he saw the smashed face of the compass. "Where's the map?" Green looked sheepishly at the broken glass but shook his head. He had no idea where the map was. It could have blown away, or fallen into the bog. He did not know and despite their searching they couldn't find it. Evans even wondered if Green had got rid of it on purpose, for now they were really stuck and might have to call for help.

Once again Green and Evans found themselves having to explain themselves to an unimpressed Parson. It didn't help that he was cold, wet and covered in mud and somehow had found a way to blame them for this fact too. Evans wanted to remind him that he had been warned but decided that now was not the time. They had to move on to work out what to do next and that would only happen after Parson finished ranting. The options were limited. They discussed the possibility of using the sun to work out the northerly direction and to just head that way, but without a map or compass, Evans argued that going on was out of the question and with Parson only having one shoe and Green's sprained ankle traversing the heather again was highly risky. Evans wondered if Parson would have taken the risk if it hadn't been him missing a shoe. In the end, they agreed that calling the emergency services was their only option.

Frustrated beyond belief Parson was not yet prepared to give up on the day's quest. He separated himself from the other two so that he could think. He knew he was at his best under pressure; all he needed to do was stay calm and work out how to play this. Staring into the middle distance his plan B quickly came together. It was obvious really, they would simply say that they were out looking for the pair of fugitives following on from their enquiries yesterday that the local force had been informed about. They hadn't wanted to wait for the usual protocols because they were concerned for the young child's safety in this obviously dangerous terrain. Genius! He congratulated himself. He might even get the helicopter to fly over this so called Charlie's Cave and flush them out. Not as good as the original plan but given the abilities of his team mates, or indeed lack of them, it was the best that could be done. It did not occur to him that it was as much down to him as the others that they were unable to continue the rest of the walk. In his own mind, it was all down to Green's failure again.

Evans was quite relieved at the prospect of a helicopter rescue. A walk through the hills had seemed a reasonable idea at breakfast but he had assumed that the other two had realised what would be involved. When it was apparent that they didn't, he'd known that some sort of accident was inevitable. He'd had to scramble half way along the plateau in order to get a phone signal to call 999. Being in a distinctive area and from what he could remember from the map, he was able to give an approximate location as he was on the only flat spot that he could see for miles around. He was told that the Coast Guard helicopter would be sent. Assuming it could find them, they had a twenty minute wait.

It was about half an hour later when they first saw the helicopter circling. Green was concerned that it had not spotted them as it appeared to fly away, but it obviously had, as soon after Evans received a text message from the Coastguard. "They say they have landed nearby and a team are on their way to join us," he updated the others.

Parson had been sitting a little apart from his colleagues. He stood up and came in closer. "Ok, let me do the talking about our business here...Just agree with what I say." That suited the other two absolutely fine, neither of them had any intention of attempting to explain what was going on.

Presently three figures appeared over the horizon.

"Smurfs in high vis, that's all we need," muttered Evans. Green smirked. They were wearing blue overalls with bright yellow jackets and hard hats. The legend HMCG was printed in large black letters.

The HMCG party consisted of a pilot, Crewman, and the Benbecula Station Officer, Howard Major. The crewman started immediately to treat Green's ankle, while Major, introducing himself as the Officer in Charge of the incident started taking details of what had happened. Parson confirmed that he was the senior police officer and gave his explanation. Major listened carefully, making the odd scribble in his notebook. He did not interrupt Parson, but when the policeman had finished, he asked politely if he could clarify a couple of points.

Firstly, he asked all three officers to produce their warrant cards to confirm identities and provide the relevant staff and branch identification numbers. Once he had written all of these down in his notebook, he then asked details of the people they were looking for. To Parson's irritation, Major knew Matt well as he was an ex-Coastguard volunteer. He was able to assure the policeman that he was very unlikely to be lost or stranded in the local terrain.

Speaking quietly but firmly, he told Parson that he understood that it was an "informal search", making the speech marks with his fingers to emphasise that he was repeating what he had been told but emphasised that according to all emergency services procedures they still should have written a search plan, undertaken a risk assessment and notified independent bodies of their planned route and objectives.

When Parson started to prevaricate, and tell him that he would get them in due course, Major began to have serious doubts about what he was being told. Professional courtesy prevented him from calling the policemen liars, yet he couldn't fathom what they could really have been up to. ...but this wasn't any normal police procedure that he had ever come across. He made a mental note to ask Florence about them. As Green's injury was minor, the crewman had treated it quickly and had been listening to Parson's explanation and was as incredulous as Major was and couldn't help asking:

"And how exactly did you three think you were going to rescue Matt, a woman and baby if they were hurt without notifying or involving anyone else?" He had no qualms about asking embarrassing questions.

Parson waffled about only wanting to call in help if it was needed, but wasn't very convincing. His colleagues had remained unhelpfully silent. He didn't want Green to say anything but he thought Evans might have helped him out.

Howard Major spent several minutes making more copious notes. Another fucking report thought Parson. The man and his thoroughness were really getting on his nerves but he had to try and keep him on side. Eventually they were ready to board the helicopter. The pilot explained that they would be flying back to Balivanich Airport, where they could make arrangements to retrieve their car. Parson asked, as politely as he could muster, about their route and whether they would be able to fly over Corrodale Bay. Major didn't see the point in this, as flying time is expensive and limited and pointed out that the Coastguard didn't normally make sightseeing detours. If the Police wanted to undertake an aerial search they could use their own helicopter he suggested. But Parson persisted. He took the point that Matt could look after himself, but what about the girl and child? With a show of contriteness that had his colleagues gaping he admitted that they may have been rushed, possibly ill advised to set out as they did, but it was only because they were worried about Matt and the girl and her toddler. He just wanted to sweep over the area to put all their minds at rest. Major scratched his head and crinkled his nose. All his gut instincts told him not to help these people any more than he had to, but he couldn't ignore the possibility of the young woman and child being in trouble. As it was not far off their route he could also not argue against the logic that it would be sensible to have a quick look.

He sighed and turned to the Pilot. "Can we do a quick sweep by the mouth of the cave and the beach? Mind you, if Matt is really there, I'd lay money he'd be in the other one."

The policemen exchanged puzzled glances at this, but didn't interrupt...at least they were going to have a look.

It was very cramped in the aircraft. The Pilot and the medic, who was actually the aircraft's co-pilot, were seated in the front. Green being "Injured" was put in the stretcher seat facing backwards, towards a control panel in the main cabin. Evans was seated with Major and Parson. They were all facing inwards with their legs intertwined, but all had a view out of the large windows over each other's shoulders. Major strapped them in, and distributed headsets. It was noisy and there would be no opportunity for private conversation.

The helicopter left the ground effortlessly. Within seconds they were heading towards the ancient cave. Howard explained a little of the history through the headset, and the fact that there were two caves. One, shown on the maps would be clearly visible from the air. The other, about half a mile further inland, was bigger and better hidden. It was believed by the locals to be the real hiding place of the royal fugitive. The policemen listened intently, realising the importance of this piece of local knowledge. They could have been wandering around all day and not found them.

"There it is," the coastguard pointed out of his left hand window, "can we get a bit closer?"

The aircraft turned and hovered and they could see the shingle beach and the entrance to a small cave. Pulled halfway up the beach was a small dinghy with an outboard motor. "Well, someone is visiting, but there's no sign of anyone in trouble... should we land and just investigate the other cave?" asked the pilot.

Neither Parson nor Major was keen on this idea and were happy to agree that the first priority had to be to return the injured Green to safety. Parson was keen to search further, but not in the company of the Coast Guard. Major made a mental note to check up on Matt's whereabouts, but not with this shoeless policeman breathing down his neck.

It was only a further short flight to Benbecula airport from the bay. There was a small reception committee waiting for them, made up of the Coast Guard jeep, an ambulance to take Green to hospital, and Inspector Florence Macrury ready to have a word with Parson.

Chapter 14: Law and Order

As Green was taken away by ambulance, Howard Major led the two policemen over to meet their Scottish counterpart. She was a small, well-built woman with auburn hair cut into a short bob and who wore her uniform with style and poise. She was technically the same rank as Parson, however her stance, confidence and cool demeanour, made it clear that she was the authority on this island and would be having the last word.

She had met Evans previously, but not Parson. She nodded, acknowledging the introduction and informed them that she had a car to take them back to the station. They were not given the choice as whether to join her or not, nor the opportunity to change or wash before they went. Evans ventured the suggestion that he would have to go and collect their car, but was told he could arrange that after they had spoken.

"Do you need me Flo?" asked the Coastguard.

"No thanks Howie, this is Police business. But I would like a copy of your incident report please?"

"OK, I'll be updating the station Log and Incident Report Book, so I'll email you copies."

Howie departed with a friendly wave as he headed towards his jeep. The others were shown to the Police car, a constable had opened the rear doors for them.

"Hope you're ok back there, it's where we usually put the criminals. Mind your heads," instructed Florence as she got in. She didn't smile or turn around.

It was a brief drive to the Police Station, a small building that looked like an afterthought in the council offices car park. They were led into a small reception area, which was hardly big enough for all of them. The constable slipped behind the reception desk and logged on at a computer screen. Florence opened an adjoining door.

"Wait here a moment, I'll just check the room is ready."

"Busy place," commented Parson. The constable looked up. Evans wasn't sure who the comment was directed at or if his boss was being sarcastic but he really didn't want either of them to make matters worse. "I've heard these new small stations work very well, how many cells do you have?"

"Five." answered the constable. Not really wanting to become involved in conversation with the visitors. To his relief, the Inspector returned. She held the door open and indicated that they should follow her.

They were led along a narrow corridor past an unmanned operations room to a small office with a table and three chairs. Florence sat down on one side of the table and indicated to her visitors to take the seats on the other side. She looked them up and down. Covered in mud and bruises the pair made a sorry sight. *Na oisich*, what idiots, she thought. "Better get on with it then".

She was being purposefully formal, not giving anything away. Evans began to wonder how much she knew, and if she was about to caution them. Parson tried to break the ice; they were after all fellow professionals. "Thank you for finding the time to see us Flo, I appreciate that you are busy.... er..," seeing her face tighten, he hesitated.

"Should I call you Flo, or Florence...it's just that the Coast Guard....Perhaps you are on closer terms with him!" His attempts to be friendly and jovial were definitely not working. Florence's eyes had widened and her eyebrows were practically through her fringe.

She leaned forward on her elbows. "Inspector will do fine, thank you, but I am going to do the talking first." The two men exchanged glances. Evans was worried, but Parsons just considered her rude, seeing her as no more than a nuisance.

She opened a drawer in the desk and took out an A4 manila folder. Taking glasses from her hand bag, she placed them on her nose and opened the folder. She looked over her glasses at the policemen. "Shall we begin?" It was a rhetorical question. Taking out the papers, she shuffled them and glanced at the top one.

"To be honest, it's more a matter of where to start." She turned to Evans. "I met you and the other one at Lochmaddy the other evening. No introduction or by your leave...you arrived late for the ferry, implying that you were there to arrest two people and getting the CalMac Staff to run around after you. Moaning about sheep, and full of your own self-importance. Now, I know we work for different forces, in different countries...but on what planet, in what universe is that acceptable inter-force procedure?"

She was shaking her head as she spoke. "Now I couldn't decide whether it was you or the mainland team being ignorant. Sending two officers over to screw up something that I'd have done with no bother, so I came back and tore a strip off the regional folk in Inverness, wanting to know what was so special that the local Teuchter woman couldn't be told about it....well?" She looked from one to the other. "They were as pissed off as I was because they knew nothing about any of this either!" She took a deep breath and looked at the papers in her hands.

"But what makes it even more interesting is that there's no Warrant out for Matt Macaulay, or the Manover girl...not in England, Scotland, Europe, not even any Interpol or extradition enquiries. Nobody's interested in them except you...so what the hell are you playing at?"

The impact of this otherwise respectable middle aged woman, speaking quietly, but firmly, suddenly swearing at them, took both officers aback, so they didn't respond at first. Parson was relieved that her only complaint seemed to be procedural; she wasn't going to be accusing him of anything. This could be dealt with. He decided the best approach would be to placate her, grovel a bit then get out of there. Assuming the most obsequious expression he could muster, he wrung his hands and looked plaintively at his feet.

"I am afraid you are absolutely right. I can only apologise profusely for the behaviour of my officers and any problems they may have caused. It is inexcusable." He paused.

I'm going to be sick if he carries on like this thought Evans.

"We did touch base with the Police in Glasgow. I guess they didn't inform you of our interest. We don't want to arrest Mr Macaulay, it's just that ...well, we've had very disturbing information regarding Miss Manover that we need to verify and are very concerned about what he is doing with her...it's as much for his protection...."

"That's ridiculous, have you seen the size of him?" Flo interrupted, rolling her eyes. "And actually, I've been speaking to Glasgow too. A nice young man called...." She looked down at her paper; "Jim Grey. He tells me that Matt helped them with an attempted mugging, then he and the girl left with their blessing. You didn't object then seemingly?"

"On top of that," she continued. "I've had Seonag Macaulay on the phone wanting to know why her son is being chased by the Poileas, and Sketch Macaulay chewing my ear off because one of you was pretending to be a relative of his in the bar of the Mountford Hotel last night. He's furious and consulting his solicitor!"

She thought that she wouldn't tell them everything that Jim Grey had said; she'd keep her powder dry. The Englishman looked worried, she'd keep him on the ropes, but he interrupted.

"Look, I really do understand why you are upset, this is a sensitive enquiry that has been badly handled and I will be appraising my senior officers of the problems...but in the meantime..."

Florence looked up, she wasn't taking this.

"No, I'm not finished yet. You see, once I heard about your foolhardy yomp across the heather this morning, actually from concerned hotel staff, I 'appraised' your senior officers for you. D'you know something? They too were very surprised, as they don't seem to be up to speed with your antics either." She paused for effect. Closing the folder over again, she smiled at both men, obviously on a roll now.

"So, I'm going to tell you what will be happening in the meantime. You are to meet with a

Murdo MacNeil in Glasgow tomorrow. Maybe this girl is important, eh? But he doesn't want any of you talking to her. Your flight is tomorrow afternoon?" The Londoner nodded

"In the meantime, get your car and your mate from hospital, and keep a low profile, for all our sakes." She gave them a hard look. "I wouldn't want to have to take you into protective custody..."

Parson stood, "Are you finished now?" Despite everything, he still managed to sound condescending.

"Yes, I think so," sighed Florence. She turned her attentions to Evans who was getting to his feet with far less bravado. "If you go through, Colin will drive you to your vehicle."

"Have a nice day," she smiled to herself as they left.

Parson maintained a stony silence as Colin picked up Green from the hospital, retrieved the car from the roadside at Loch Eynort and left them to drive back to the Mountford Hotel car park. Green was confused, realising that something had happened, but not being sure of the implications. Evans switched off the engine and turned to his boss.

"Well, are we going back to Glasgow tomorrow?"

"Don't be stupid." Parson was back on form. "I'm not being told what to do by that jumped up little tart."

To avoid being overheard they sat in the car to discuss their options. There was no choice really, they had to get to the girl and destroy that handbag and whatever else she had. It didn't really matter what she had told Matt; without the evidence it would be the ranting of an illegal immigrant and hearsay, although disposing of her would still be by far the best option. They needed to get back to Corrodale Bay, with the advantage of now knowing to head for the right cave. Green was keen to redeem his standing, and had been thinking things over whilst waiting for the others.

"Why don't we hire a boat....there were leaflets about it in the hotel? We can be dropped nearby, to do some sightseeing before we leave. Then just happen to bump into them....If we need to, we can use that boat we saw."

"Or call for reinforcements having been attacked by them," smiled Parson.

"It would have to look good," cautioned Evans.

"Don't worry, I can make it so." Parson was being cryptic again, but the plan was agreed. They went to hire a boat trip. Green collected a selection of the leaflets in the hotel foyer for local boats, while Evans looked up the Visit Scotland site on line, to see if he could find a boat hire company a little further afield, who might not be so friendly with the local authorities.

~~~
~~~

Chapter 15: Charlie's Cave

Matt couldn't believe his eyes, he felt sick with frustration and disappointment as he threw himself into the heather to avoid being seen. The Coast Guard Helicopter! What was that doing here.....and how did Parson manage to get himself into it? He'd left Marieke and Kazik and was on his way to check that the dinghy was still ok on the shingle beach. As the aircraft headed towards him. there were no trees or pylons to obstruct its pass so it was able to come down very low. It couldn't have been much more than 100 feet above his head and Matt had a clear view of the passengers. He could see Howie Major with Parson sitting next to him. Matt was confused and alarmed. As far as he was concerned Parson and his cronies should still be in Fort William or Glasgow. Not here, not yet. Had they got hold of Kate? Had Murdo betrayed them? What was going on?

What really bugged him as he watched it fly away was that he'd let himself think that they'd got Parson beaten. Kate would be in Glasgow by now, all they'd had to do was sit tight for a little longer but they'd been tracked down again. He was gutted.

It had all been going so well too. He hadn't been sure at first if Marieke had understood what he had meant by "camping", and what it would entail but she had helped enthusiastically when they picked up supplies and cooking equipment. She had encouraged Kazik and been quite excited as they set out in Callum's boat. Far easier by boat than coming at it from the west, mused Matt, not knowing that the route was even then being tested. Marieke and Kazik were tougher and more practical than they looked but that was probably how they'd survived, he supposed. They had passed the small cave on the beach, and then followed a sheep trail up the rise in the heather. The cave was well camouflaged, and unless you knew it was there you could hardly see it until you were almost upon it, and even then you had to look hard. There was a deceptively small opening in the rock, which opened up into a spacious dry and sheltered refuge inside. They worked cheerfully together to build their camp, finding natural sleeping and cooking areas. This will do, he thought. He could see how the Jacobites had found safety here.

He'd built a fire using driftwood collected on the beach, and they'd cooked a supper of beans and hotdogs, washed down with some Morgan's Spiced Rum which they sipped as the sun set. The few clouds turned a magical fluffy pink; tinting the whole sky with their aura, warming the whole landscape. We deserve a break, he thought. As they were in the middle of nowhere he wasn't able to use the translation app on the phone, so they had resorted largely to drawing pictures, miming and waving their arms around. Just as dusk was falling, Matt realised that they had company. He nudged Marieke, bringing his finger to his lips, then pointing out toward the hills. On a nearby ridge, silhouetted against the sunset there was a family of deer. The stag with antlers towering into the sky, and a hind and her fawns looking beautifully innocent were staring towards their campfire.

"They're probably wondering what we're doing here," he whispered.

Night fell and as the storm of the previous day finally passed the sky revealed a breath-taking view of the stars and planets. Marieke was mesmerised and stood for ages staring at the heavens and pointing at the stars and the moon with her son. Matt drew a crude diagram of the sun and planets to explain Saturn and Jupiter among the stars. They laughed as they tried to work out the various constellations.

Matt knew it would get cold overnight under the clear sky, so he opened up the two sleeping bags they had bought and zipped them together. As he laid them on the camping mats he tried to explain that their body heat would keep them warm. He was not sure that she understood, but she didn't object to the concept of them sleeping so close. As they snuggled up next to the embers of the fire with Kazik between them, Marieke whispered, "thank you" as she fell asleep with her head on his shoulder. He'd lain still, holding both of them, feeling relaxed, breathing in the comforting smells of mother and child. It was strange but despite the extreme situation, he'd felt more content than he had done in months.

The following morning went well. The sun shone as Matt cooked breakfast. Kazik ate everything that was put in front of him, including some things he shouldn't have. But the upshot was that he was more awake and livelier than he had been over the last few days. Marieke seemed pleased; it looked as if he was beginning to recover from his ordeal. They walked in the hills to see if they could see the deer again, but as Matt expected, there was no sign of them. Instead, they were delighted by a display from two eagles, soaring above the ridge. It was as if the wildlife were checking them out. They didn't think that they could be warning of intruders. In the afternoon they went down to the beach, played in the shallows and marvelled at the variety of bird life. Matt wondered if they could take the dinghy and try fishing. Could he fashion some homemade fishing lines, he wondered. It was as if they were on holiday. Neither of them spoke of Parson, or murder...they just recharged their batteries. Kazik was fascinated by the waves and inevitably ended up in the water. His mother slipped while playing in the shallows and they both got very wet. It was while she was drying him off in the cave that Matt had decided to go back further along the bay to check the boat. It was the approaching sound of the rotors that had caused him to drop into the heather and burrow as deep as he could.

Once he was sure they'd gone he sat up in the grass. He just wanted to swear and kick and punch something, but he knew he had to calm down. Someone must have blabbed; they must have tricked Howie, and he would have told the story of the two caves.

"Bastards!" He shouted after the helicopter.

No Macaulay; stop panicking and think...What are they going to do next? He was fairly sure that he hadn't been seen... Would they come back by boat to try and surprise them? That's what he would do. He started back towards the cave. As he climbed the hill he became more and more convinced that they had to move. But where to? He knew he had a couple of hours, because they would have to return to Balivanich and rent some sort of craft, if they were going to come back. Looking at his watch, he thought they probably wouldn't be able to do that today...not in daylight...would they come in the dark? They had in Glasgow and Fort William, it would be mad, but he couldn't risk it. He was in too much of a hurry to follow the path, so he clambered up the hill side, running through the options in his mind as he climbed. They could walk out west, through the hills, but he discounted that because it was quite an arduous slog. It would be dark by the time they reached the main road and he would probably have to carry Kazik for most of the way. No, their only choice was to take the little boat round to the Pier at Loch Carnan to the north while it was still light. There was a chance that they'd meet the coppers he thought, but at least there would be people about. If they left quickly they could get there before them. He wasn't sure where they would go after that. He had an idea about hiding in one of the old military bunkers on the South Uist Rocket Range. It would be defendable and he could summon help from there. He had calmed down and was thinking as a Marine, they'd be ok. All that remained was to explain it to Marieke... again.

Like Matt, Marieke had managed to calm down at least a little since arriving at Corrodale Bay. Perhaps it was the sea air, or just managing to sleep without being afraid...but she felt different. She sang to Kazik as she dried him, thinking that maybe, there could really be an end to her nightmare.

But she knew it wasn't as soon as she saw Matt approach. There was something in his stance that told her something was seriously wrong. She put Kazik down.

"What?" She asked "What is it?" Their eyes met. He looked very sad.

"Parson," he growled. Her blood ran cold.

"Here?" she gasped.

"No...in the Coast Guard helicopter." She didn't understand. "A Plane" he repeated, then started flapping his arms and swaying from side to side. She smiled and shook her head despite herself. "We have to go," he told her. She understood this, nodding as she started to gather things together. He reached out and touched her arm. "No, just what we need." She stared at him confused. He pointed at the nappy bag and the child, "That's it....We leave everything else." She understood; they had to go quickly.

When Callum had sailed them round the previous evening in his fishing boat; it had taken about an hour. They had towed the little dinghy with an outboard motor for emergency use. Not thinking that it would actually be used, they didn't have any life jackets. Although the weather had improved, the sea was still choppy from the previous day's storm. There were

Bungee ropes in the bottom of the craft. Matt used these to physically tie Kazik to his mother and to secure both of them to the boat.

"Keep low and hold on tight" he told her, miming how he wanted her to sit in the boat. She agreed, looking slightly apprehensive. "We'll keep close to the shore, take it steady, and we should be OK." He was reassuring himself as much as Marieke.

He knew the route well enough; he and Callum had kayaked around here many a time as children. He needed to sail as far as Ushnish lighthouse, past the bay that led into the old ruined Skipport pier and round to the small harbour and slipway at Loch Carnan. His concern was the swell, not just losing a passenger, but it would hold them up, and increase the chances of running into the southerners. He had debated simply pulling into Skipport pier. It was a more sheltered bay, surrounded as it was by the South Uist hills. But the old pier was abandoned and eroded. It would make an interesting climb, especially with a small child and the precious bag. Weighing up the options, he also thought that it wouldn't be a good idea if they were to meet up with Parson and his crew in a deserted bay. God knows what might happen. Despite the distance and sea state Loch Carnan was the better option, there would be people about and even the chance or picking up a lift if they were very lucky.

It took them just under the hour to sail around the headland, but to Marieke it felt like a life time. She'd never been in such a small boat before and felt tiny and vulnerable against the wrath of the sea. At first, she thought it was a bit odd that Matt had tied them in but as they were bounced around and thrown about the boat, she was very glad that he had. She had no idea what to expect and started crying, believing they were going to drown as the first spray soaked them in the boat. Matt tried to reassure her but with little success, until he could point to where they intended to land. She was getting tired of the chase. The fact that they had been found again had really knocked her spirit. Feeling so sick and defenceless, she was about ready to give up.

The swell calmed as they approached the inlet. Matt decided to beach the dinghy on the commercial vessel slipway rather than sail all the way around to the busy harbour. That way he would be able to approach land away from the car park, so would be less likely to be spotted by outgoing craft. Also, it gave Marieke a chance to pull herself together before they met anyone.

They pulled Callum's dinghy out of the way, then started toward the main buildings. Close to three large wind turbines that dominated the landscape, the pier was an unlikely local hub. It was home to "Scottish Fuels", the main supplier of heating oil for the islands; the smoke house for Salar Salmon, a tourist attraction for the foodie types as well as being the access point to the Minch for local fishermen and tourists alike. It was early evening and there were a number of cars parked outside the various buildings. Matt's plan was to "borrow" a vehicle. As it was such a small community, most locals were in the habit of leaving their car keys in the car...if not in the ignition itself. Matt was looking to see if there was a vehicle he recognised, a car belonging to somebody who would forgive him afterwards. He smiled when he realised they were in luck. Parked outside the fuel office was the distinctive people carrier belonging to his cousin Sketch. He knew it would cost him several drams, but Sketch wouldn't mind when he knew the whole story.

He turned to guide Marieke towards the building, when a familiar voice called "Oy... I've been looking for you ....Have ye any idea how much bother ye're in laddie?"

~~~
~~~

Chapter 16: Going Home

Marieke's body froze, while her eyes darted from left to right, trying to glimpse Parson or one of his goons. She clutched her child tightly, convinced that this day was going to be her last. Matt took her by the elbow, and steered her towards the people carrier taxi, "Just keep walking", he muttered. It was one of those odd situations, where he knew and recognised the voice, but couldn't see the speaker. He didn't want a big reunion on the quayside. It was Sketch, but where was he? A man his size wasn't usually hard to spot. He propelled Marieke even faster, he didn't want to stop and explain himself in full view and he should get her and Kazik into the car if nothing else.

Thankfully Sketch was thinking along the same lines, He was emerging from the shop door of the Salar Salmon smoke house, carrying two large boxes. His sense of balance and agility were quite impressive for a large man. He looked furtive. Matt wondered what he was up to, then realised he was being cautious and looking round on his behalf.

"Quick, into the car!" he called. Matt smiled and complied. He didn't bother explaining his original plan. Sketch put his boxes in the boot then climbed in, shutting the door behind him. He looked Marieke and Kazik up and down as they sat nervously on his back seat. He'd heard the stories about there being a woman and child with Matt, "S'all right, you dinnae need to be feared of me, lassie." He smiled. She didn't understand a word he said, but appreciated his friendly tone and kind eyes, so couldn't help smiling back.

Turning to Matt he took his hand and shook it. "And am I glad to see you laddie? D'you ken there's a bunch of English Poileas looking for you and claiming to be related to us? What have you done?" Matt laughed. Only Sketch could make the description "English" sound quite so insulting.

"Would you believe nothing? Actually, I'm meant to be helping the Glasgow Poileas, but it's all got kind of out of hand. We just need to stay out of the way for a couple of days. Can you take us down to the Range? I thought I might shack up in one of their old storage buildings."

"No! I'm taking you home. Your mam has been going spare."

"You don't understand, these guys are dangerous, I don't want them near Mam or Iona."

"Last I heard, Flo Macrury was having a wee chat with them. She's mightily pissed off by all accounts, so bound to sort them out. That's one woman I wouldnae want tae annoy."

He chuckled as he started the engine and manoeuvred the car out of the car park, past the turbines, acknowledging a couple of other drivers as they passed. "The word will be out that we have been seen." Matt thought. Flo may try to sort things out, but the reason they were here was because Jim Grey and his boss couldn't pin the southerners down. He hadn't decided whose side Murdo MacNeil was on and he needed to find out if Kate had managed to speak with him to sort things out but Florence would at least keep Parson busy in the meantime and buy them a few hours.

They turned onto the main road and headed south. It was normally about a twenty minute drive to Bornish but there was a lot of traffic heading north, causing them to stop at every other passing place. "There's an exercise on, they've got visitors, so you wouldnae get onto the Range anyway," noted Sketch. "They got us running round all over the place. You wouldnae believe it, but that's who I had to pick up the salmon for, *tha eri mor as a fhein*...the posh eejits." The military visitors to what was locally referred to as the "Rocket Range" did provide business and employment for the community but their secretive nature and apparently odd priorities made them a frequent source of amusement.

Marieke wasn't really listening to the conversation; she was intrigued by another aspect of South Uist. Every time they slowed down or stopped she noticed what looked like small shrines on the side of the road. She wasn't sure at first. They were white boxes with a figure inside that looked vaguely familiar. But when they stopped closer to one she was able to get a better look. She felt strangely emotional recognising the figure of the Madonna and child with fresh flowers at her feet. It brought back memories of her family, childhood and home. Her own mother used to pray to the Madonna, was she praying for her now? She hoped so, she missed her so much.

As they pulled up to the house the kitchen door opened and Seonag Macaulay came out. She looked vaguely disappointed. "I'm waiting for the midwife, Peggy Walker, have you seen her?" The question was directed at Sketch. She was obviously pre-occupied because she didn't even notice Matt in the car. Her eyebrows rose and her body stiffened as he opened the passenger door. "Oh, it's you, is it? We need to talk young man; but I don't have time right now. Your sister is really not well."

Sketch winked, and mouthed "good luck" as they got out of the car. He offered to drive Iona to hospital. But Seonag wanted to wait for the Midwife. She ushered Matt and his guests into the house, while she tried to phone her again.

Seonag couldn't stay mad at Matt for long, she'd been so worried when he seemed to disappear off the planet, with all the strange stories going around about him being chased by the police, she was just relieved that he was home safe and well. Like other Uist women she was able to cope with most things and not easily panicked but having her son going missing while her daughter was ill had raised her stress levels and sharpened the tongue. Seeing the midwife's car heading along the road towards the house she began to feel less anxious about her daughter and able to deal with other things such as her troublesome son.

Matt had wanted to speak with his sister, but his mother had put him off until after the home visit. Finally, Peggy Walker, the midwife, arrived. There were normally two midwives to service the whole of the chain of islands from Berneray to Eriskay but unfortunately Peggy's counterpart was off sick, so she was covering the whole area herself until relief arrived, which meant a lot of running about. After a brief hello, she was shown upstairs to Iona. Seonag joined Matt and Marieke in the kitchen.

"Kettle's on, mum." She nodded her thanks and sat down at the table. Looking at her son, he seemed weary. The girl with him looked like a scared rabbit, all wide eyed and fidgety. The child looked dirty and skinny, but contented. He was happily sucking on a finger of shortbread that Matt had given him. Can't be good for his teeth, she thought.

"We've got some yogurt or fruit, if you want him to have something a bit healthier," she offered. Marieke didn't quite understand and looked at Matt questioningly.

"It's ok, we can get to that," Matt replied "We need to explain what's going on, well, as much as we can, we don't have much time." His mother was obviously surprised at Matt answering for Marieke regarding her child. "Marieke doesn't speak much English, she's Romanian...speaks a little Polish though."

"I see," replied his mother, not really seeing at all. "You'd better start at the beginning and keep it simple then." Sitting down opposite her, Matt gave her a mug of tea and began to explain, starting with the attack outside the Park Bar. He described how Murdo MacNeil had asked him to help keep the girl safe in Glasgow, while the police were investigating Parson and his men but how they had decided to head to the islands when it became clear that the English thugs were not so easy to shake off. He didn't mention murder, vice, or being chased for stolen evidence; he thought it would just complicate matters. He told her how Kate had gone back to Glasgow to make contact with Murdo, and they were just waiting for one of them to let them know when it would be safe to bring Marieke back to the city. He'd done as he had been asked, and kept it simple.

Both his mother and Marieke listened closely to his explanation. He did not know how much Marieke understood, he hadn't explained to her that they had known Murdo and that he was acting on his behalf. His mother asked why he had not come straight home instead of camping out in the wild. Although she didn't push it, her facial expression showed that she considered his explanation of not wanting to bother his sick sister as rather lame. She'd heard that Florence Macrury was talking to the visitors, so couldn't really see why he was in such a rush or what the problem was.

Seonag was going to question him further, but stopped in her tracks as she heard Iona's bedroom door open and close. Peggy didn't come down stairs immediately; she was speaking on the phone. Seonag stood up. "You need to phone Father Ross." It was an instruction.

"Mum?" Matt was confused "Why on earth d'you need a priest? She's not that sick surely?"

"No, not for me, for you and her!" Seonag was pointing at Marieke.

"What are you going on about? Have you not been listening? Why would we need a priest?" He began to wonder what gossip his mam had been listening to and if she was losing it with the stress.

They could hear Peggy moving about on the landing upstairs now. Seonag was feeling equally exasperated with her son. She rolled her eyes, "I'm not saying anything about your relationship! I know you haven't been in a while, but if you remember the sign outside St. Mary's Church, Father Ross speaks seven languages, several of which are Eastern European. I don't know about Romanian but I'm fairly sure he speaks Polish. After that, I want you to phone Kate."

"Yes, ok I will. But will you tell me now, what's wrong with Iona?"

"Oh Matt, I'm so worried." His mother's eyes had moistened and there was a crack in her voice as she spoke quickly.

"Peggy came on Monday for her check-up after you left. She really wasn't happy with her. Her blood pressure is still high, and she is simply not resting enough. The swelling in her ankles had gone, so she thought she was fine, but it's back now. As she's getting close to thirty six weeks, Peggy told her to pack a bag. Just in case. Iain can't get back because of the weather and that's not helping her stay calm, nor did your disappearance!" It wasn't a jibe, just a statement of fact. Matt leaned over and took his mother's hands.

"C'mon Mam, it'll be fine...it's that stubborn bloody mindedness that will see her and the baby through. Maybe she'll be better off in Glasgow? She'll have no choice but to rest in the Southern General and it'll be easier for Iain to get there."

The kitchen door opened. Seonag turned to see Peggy standing in the doorway. She looked and sounded worryingly serious. "We need to have a few quiet words *math tha.*"

Matt suggested that he and Marieke go and have their own few quiet words with his sister to give them privacy. Peggy agreed, but warned him not to tire her out.

Iona looked pale and weak lying in the bed. She smiled as her brother came in, and couldn't resist teasing him. "You've got a nerve turning up here Macaulay after dumping mine and Kate's cars. Lucky for you, I can't get up to thump you."

They both laughed, although he was alarmed that she seemed to have deteriorated in just a week. Sitting on the bed he held her hand and introduced Marieke and Kazik. They talked quietly as they compared the events of the week, and the options left for Matt and Marieke. Matt kept his adventures light hearted, but did ask his sister a favour.

The conversation between Peggy and Seonag was more serious. The midwife explained that she had called for the air ambulance. A local ambulance would be here shortly to take them to the airport in Benbecula to meet it. Iona's blood pressure was now over one hundred, there were traces of protein in her urine and the oedema was getting worse on both her ankles and hands. It wasn't life threatening yet. Had they been on the mainland she would have been seen as a hospital outpatient, but in South Uist there simply weren't the facilities, so they had to err on the side of caution. After thirty six weeks, she wouldn't be allowed to fly on a scheduled flight; they just couldn't take the risk of Iona deteriorating and being stranded. Seonag understood; she felt somewhat relieved that her daughter would be looked after in hospital.

"Can I go with her?" she asked.

Peggy thought about this.

"It depends; we need to head to the hospital now. I was going to ask the doctors to prescribe hyper-tension drugs for the journey. As it is, I should accompany her... but I don't want to leave the islands without cover. If her blood pressure comes down enough, then you could go with the paramedic, but that really does depend how she is. Let's just keep her as calm as possible."

They were interrupted by Peggy's phone ringing. She stepped outside to receive the call and when she came back into the house it was with the news that the ambulance was on its way. Seonag went to tell her daughter the news and throw together her own overnight bag. She offered to fetch her daughter's belongings. She couldn't recall Iona having such a mismatch of scruffy bags. But Iona wanted things left as they were.

"Matt will get the bags, just get your own stuff." Seonag thought this odd, but went along with it so as not to stress her further.

Seonag and Matt were together in the kitchen when the ambulance arrived. She was busy giving her son instructions regarding the croft, and who to contact about their trip to hospital. Iona sat by the fire, holding her bag and talking to Kazik, who was next to her on his mother's lap. The two girls seemed to be getting on, despite the language barrier. As she rose to leave the house Matt took the bag from her.

"I'll carry this," he smiled.

He hugged his mother and sister tightly. "Let me know how you get on," he reminded them. Both women nodded, but for different reasons as the ambulance drove away to the airport.

When they returned to the kitchen, Matt tried to phone Kate using his mobile, but just like Peggy, he couldn't get any mobile phone signal. Blow it, he thought, Mum will have her on speed dial. He was pleased to get through quickly and gave a brief update as to Iona's condition, and that she was on her way to the Southern General. He confirmed that it was more precautionary than dangerous but was more anxious to learn how Kate had got on in Glasgow. Had she talked to Murdo? Kate confirmed that she had but Matt knew it wasn't good news as soon as his sister started swearing in Gaelic. Ever since they were children that was not usually a good sign.

~~~
~~~

Chapter 17: No place to hide

Kate described how she had managed to track down PC Jim Grey, who put her in contact with Murdo MacNeil.

"It was.., oh I don't know... *ith chac*, all shit," she exclaimed. "They saw me at the same police station that you must have been at. They took the copies of Marieke's statement but then kept me waiting while they deliberated over it. Don't worry I've kept one for myself. Murdo and Jim, with this rude English git, who didn't introduce himself, asked loads of questions. Curiously though, they didn't ask where you are at the moment. They did ask if I knew Florence Macrury, which makes me think that they probably do know where you are. Finally, without a by your leave, they formally thanked me for the information but said that it was, "all hearsay"! The Sasannach amadan, *English idiot* said that Marieke had not claimed to see the man that left the room with her friend; "She actually stated that she was hiding under the blanket," he read in his poxy accent...so couldn't have seen him. He then went on to say that as for the other woman who she claims was hurt, there were no reports of any other female casualties in the area. MacNeil just sat quietly while this was going on. Then the interview was ended abruptly by the un-named blaigeard who went on to lecture me that Marieke was potentially the witness to a crime and more than likely involved in illegal immigration and unlawful activities herself. That you, Matt, had made yourself an accessory to her activities... he told me to tell you that aiding and abetting a criminal was an offence too. That you should hand yourselves into the nearest police station and things would be taken from there. He reckoned it would put you in a better position if you did so voluntarily. I was not impressed with him, his sympathy or his bloody reckoning!

MacNeil escorted me out of the building. When we were alone he confided that Inspector Parson had been invited to join him at a meeting in Glasgow. He suggested that Marieke and you shouldn't hand yourselves in until you know that Parson is somewhere else. Too right! But I don't know who was in charge, him or the English blaigeard, and I didn't like the fact that he kept quiet about getting you involved in the first place. Hope he isn't going to hang you out to dry." She was furious at the *"nach iad tha mor as do fein*, posh idiots, and being dismissed so rudely. Matt, although disappointed, was not surprised. It had occurred to him that Parson had to have friends in high places in order to get away with what he had done so far. The question was: was Murdo one of them?

"Don't worry; I think we have the evidence. It was in her baby bag all along. That's why I think they are chasing her." Marieke watched as he paced around the kitchen. "I don't like it that they're here. It'll take too long to explain now, but I've thought of a way to get the evidence to Glasgow. But we're sitting ducks here... going to have to hide again. I was thinking of the old Chapel house in the village. I think it's empty right now. We'll stay there till we hear they've gone. You go see Iona. Let me know if you hear anything."

"Be careful *Math tha...*" she started to tell him that she cared for him, but he interrupted.

"I know, I know... Go see Iona and mum. We'll talk soon." He hung up.

Marieke once again knew from Matt's tone, body language and the sadness in his eyes when he looked at her that the conversation with Kate had not gone as he had hoped.

"They not believe me?" It was half question, half statement.

"They need evidence," he replied flatly. She looked puzzled.

"The bag...."

"Ah, I understand. What do we do now?"

"Hide."

"Camping again?" She looked and sounded rather uneasy. He guessed that she didn't relish the prospect of traipsing up the side of a hill again in the dark.

"No," he smiled. "No more camping."

He was having difficulty finding a signal to use his phone, so using his laptop, he found the translation website Kate had used. He told her that there was an empty house at the bottom of the village that belonged to the church, it had been renovated to attract tourists, but was not being used at the moment. They could walk there. He had helped to decorate it and knew where the spare key was kept.

"We can stay there a couple of days and nobody will know. Parson will go away and we will be safe."

"What about your mother...she will worry?" She grimaced, miming a frowning face. Kazik laughed.

"She's going to be in Glasgow with the girls. Kate will tell her. She will help talk to the police."

Marieke nodded, then leant over to the keyboard and typed.

"Does the house have a bed and a shower?"

"Yes," nodded Matt, "But," he typed, "We must go soon. They will know where I live and could come here at any time. We can take all we need from here."

Dusk was falling as they started out, so they had to use torches to follow the road through the village then up a lane to the old manse house. It was a large white mock Tudor structure. Built originally in the 1930s of large stone blocks that were hewn and shaped from local boulders. Originally planned as part of an ecclesiastical expansion, the church's plans changed with the advent of war, so it became redundant. It was not until the early twenty first century that the local Parish Priest, with the help of his congregation, restored it to its original splendour, putting it to use for the local community. Marieke thought it was beautiful, even before they went inside. Matt was quietly relieved when the key was still hidden under a stone by the back steps. Once inside, Marieke was even more enchanted. The grand staircase and high ceilings were from a romantic time gone by, yet it was equipped with all the modern conveniences. It didn't take long to switch the heating on and settle themselves into the kitchen. Matt ended up making several trips back to his mother's house. Partly to check for unwanted visitors but also to pick up little luxuries such as some wine and cakes...well, they might as well enjoy themselves. He used his torch sparingly, so as not to attract attention but it was needed as he went back and forth, for although the house had been restored, the track up to it was littered with potholes that were treacherous in the dark. When in the house, they made sure that all the curtains were drawn before they turned on the lights. He felt a bit paranoid. This was South Uist after all and Father Michael probably wouldn't mind him being there anyway... but right now he felt justified in being suspicious.

It was after several uneventful checks of his mother's house, and the best part of a bottle of wine, that they began to feel a little more relaxed. Settling Kazik under a blanket on one of the large sofas in the drawing room, Marieke and Matt went into the kitchen, where they used the laptop to help them communicate. Sitting together on a small sofa by the stove they began discussing their predicament, but just kept going round in circles. Matt really hoped that they had finally managed to disappear this time and that all they had to do was sit it out now. Marieke really wanted to believe him. They started to listen to music, he showed her photos of his travels and told her a little of his illness. They joked and reminisced about happier times, getting to know the Matt and Marieke outside the nightmare. Although they came from different worlds, they had a lot in common. The same passions and prejudices, even the same dry wit. They cuddled more out of comfort than desire but each was aware of the other's presence and the potential for another kind of relationship in different circumstances. They didn't share these thoughts, but were content that they both could feel it. Finally, having talked themselves out and drunk more than they should, they snuggled up and fell asleep in front of the fire.

Back in the Mountford Hotel, Evans and Parson were sitting in their usual spot. After dinner, Evans had returned to his room to, "Catch up with things", but also to give himself some space from the other two.

Washed and rested after their ordeal in the hills, they had pretty much physically recovered, but both harboured feelings of discontent after the afternoon's activities. Green had always known that his boss was cold and ruthless and for a time he had benefited from this. Still, he was worried that things had gone too far. He had heard Parson bragging about "getting rid of people" who had got in his way before. He'd known about people who had been moved, framed or just bullied out of the way but this was in a whole different league. Shutting up the nosey little tart who had caused all this trouble was one thing, but doing away with a kid was another. What was the game plan going to be at the beach if they'd found them? They were just going to leave the kid to be found back in Glasgow. This was different. Thinking back to how Parson was behaving, he realised that everyone was becoming expendable and that could also include him.

Parson festered in his usual mire of discontent and loathing. He truly believed that they would not be in this situation if it wasn't for the complete idiocy and incompetence of his men. They had a nice little scheme going. Not too ambitious, making money and ensnaring the right people. Cheap anonymous whores and vulnerable, rich clients. He thought he had it made. Now he was chasing around this armpit of a place, tying up other people's loose ends and Green had the nerve to be getting squeamish on him. No. It would end here. Then his life could return to normal. Definitely without Green and possibly without Evans as well. He showed potential, and could be useful, but the dour Welshman would always be a witness.

On top of that he had had to endure a dressing down from that jumped up middle aged frump of an Inspector. It didn't cross his mind that he would have behaved in exactly the same way had the situation been reversed but he hated the fact that he had to kowtow to her. The fact that she alluded to conversations in Glasgow and that MacNeil character also unsettled him. He felt that he should know of MacNeil, but he couldn't place him. That too was not a good sign and it worried him.

He prided himself on his lateral thinking and versatility. He smiled as he recollected how it was he who came up with the alternate plan to hire a boat. Another potentially neat solution! The frustration returned though, because, despite a number of boat hire signs that they had seen, the Army had apparently hired them all for whatever they were doing on their training range the next day. Several skippers told Evans that if they were not needed, they would happily take them out but wouldn't be in a position to confirm till after nine in the morning. Why don't the army have their own bloody boats? What did they need them for? Why couldn't they start earlier? He had looked through his little black book of contacts to see if he knew anyone who could discreetly bring pressure to bear, but to no avail. It was another complication he didn't need.

His reverie was disturbed by somebody moving glasses on the table. He looked up, about to scowl at an unwanted interruption from the barman, when he realised it was Evans placing three drinks in front of them. He was smiling broadly.

"Thought we might like a little toast, gents, to celebrate our good news!"

His colleagues looked at him uncomprehendingly. "Oh, didn't I say? Just had an email from the surveillance team. Seems our boyo rang the sister in Glasgow... most unhappy she is, seems we have friends in the right places. Anyway, he said not to worry...told her that they have the bag, where they are keeping it and where they are now. Anyone want to see?" He placed his laptop on the table and turned the screen towards his boss and took a large slurp of his drink.

Parson devoured the information greedily, while Green read it over his shoulder. Sitting back, he asked, "D'you know where this house is?"

Never bloody satisfied; no well done, or thank you, thought Evans, but he patiently replied, "not yet, but it should be fairly easy. When you've read that, let me do a search."

Evans was as good as his word. The history and location of the manse house in Bornish was well documented. Complete with photographs of both the outside grounds and internal lay out.

"How long will it take us to get there?" was Parson's next question.

Evans and Green looked at each other.

"About half an hour we think?" suggested Green.

"Let's call it an hour then," retorted his boss. "Right, now listen carefully; we are going to pay them a little visit in the middle of the night...at three in the morning to be precise. When they are nicely tucked up in bed, thinking they are safe and not expecting us. We meet at the car at two am...don't be late." He glared at Green. "So, don't stay here too long but make sure you say good night to a couple of people to be noticed." He nodded as if accepting their agreement and left the bar, thanking the manager for a lovely dinner, en route.

"What's he like?" asked Green rhetorically, rolling his eyes.

"You better be up for this," warned Evans, "It's in all our interests!"

"Just don't get us lost this time," snarled Green as he got up.

~~~
~~~

Chapter 18: Up South

It was cold and dark at two that morning. It was darker than usual for the time of year as the moon was hidden behind a thick curtain of rain clouds. The hotel lights made very little difference to the pervading gloom. Evans, carrying a map and torch, handed the car keys to Green.

"You drive and I'll navigate, ok?" He climbed into the passenger seat as Parson settled himself into the back. "I take it we know where we are going then?"

"Sort of," quipped Evans. The other two glared at him. Parson was his usual cold self while Green looked anxious but the wiry Welshman was pleased to be finally finishing things and at the prospect of getting back to normality. "I know how to get to the village, but while there's a lot on the net about the history of the house, there is very little about how to actually find it... It's not marked as number 33 or the second on the left. We have to head south to a village called Bornish, not as far as we went yesterday. Once in the village it's a turning on the left. It's not that big a place...if we get as far as the church we've passed it. It's a mock Tudor white stone building so should be fairly easy to spot."

He made himself comfortable as Green adjusted his seat and started the engine. Parson sat back and placed the small bag he was carrying on the seat beside him.

"Ready then? Right out of the car park; then right at the T junction at the end of the road. Up South as they say round here, apparently."

They followed the main road south over the causeway from Benbecula to South Uist quite easily. The road was straight, wide and well lit. Evans was reading from the map out loud, he wanted all decisions to be shared, in an attempt to avoid being blamed for any problems. The road narrowed as they came to another smaller causeway.

"The map reckons we're crossing two lochs here...one on each side, but I can't pronounce either of them."

Neither of the others was really interested. Moving into the countryside the road dipped and rose again as they travelled towards the hills they had walked through the previous day.

"It looks different in the dark," commented Green. Evans silently agreed. The night had fallen around the little car like a thick blanket, masking any familiar points of reference, signs or even the shape of the road ahead. Green was driving more slowly than usual. He was unnerved by Parson's brooding presence in the back of the car; his mood seemed to be fed by the all-consuming darkness that enveloped them.

Parson was suddenly leaning forward. "What the hell is that?" He was pointing to an array of lights to the right, which looked like some sort of industrial complex. "We didn't pass that yesterday." He sounded worried, which wasn't like him. His colleagues both noticed.

"Yes, we did, but it wasn't all lit up," explained Evans. It's the Ministry of Defence testing place. They call it the Rocket Range, it's not that noticeable during the day."

"I'd notice rockets being fired," laughed Green. He felt better knowing that Parson was as on edge as the rest of them.

His levity did not last however as they drove away from the lights. The road became narrow and winding, with sharp bends and dips that seemed to disappear in front of him.

"We'll be quicker walking if you go much slower," came the jibe from the back seat. But Green ignored him, he could drive if he wanted to, he thought, but he wasn't going any faster. His caution was rewarded a little further on. As he drove out of a bend the road widened ahead and he was about to speed up when he spotted the gleam of what looked like small green lights. There seemed to be a number of them, and they were moving. "What the...?" Parson couldn't comprehend what he was seeing.

"Sheep!" Came the chorus from the front. "We told you this place was wild at night," muttered Green, as he tried to manoeuvre around the flock. The sheep were just meandering in the road. It was so dark that they could only make out the silhouettes of those on the verge and couldn't see which direction they were heading. Green hit the horn in an attempt to scare them off, this made the flock more frantic for a couple of minutes and eventually they passed them.

"Tasty looking lambs there," laughed Evans. "If you hit one, we'll put it in the boot. Make a nice roast that!"

Shouldn't think we'll get it on the plane though, he chuckled to himself.

Eventually, Evans told them that the turning for Bornish should be coming up soon. They spotted it and turned right onto an even smaller side road. They could not see anything, other than the inky blackness of water on either side of them. None of the houses were visible from the road in the dark. "This might take a while," grunted the Welshman. "Let's stop a minute and have a think. It's up a lane on the left coming from the main road. I think we are going to have to go back, and try going up each one till we find it."

"You're joking," moaned Green.

"Got a better idea?"

"We will have to turn the car lights off, it will give us the element of surprise and avoid disturbing any neighbours if we do go down a wrong path," agreed Parson.

Green complained, but was told to just get on with it. They turned the car around and inched along the road in the dark, all of them expecting to hit something. They didn't even dare speak as Green made cautious three point turns in front of a couple of farm houses. They all froze as a dog started barking at one of the cottages, but no lights came on. They left quickly.

At the second house, they couldn't find the building because it was so dark. There was no drive as such, just a grassy track, flattened by the owners' vehicles. Impatiently, Parson snapped at the driver to turn around, but to his dismay, they couldn't see or work out the direction they had come from. Parson's mellifluous hissing was all that Green could hear as he found his way to the boundary fence and drove along next to it, until he found the gap through which they had come in. They made two further wrong house calls before they found the track they wanted.

It was only a few hundred yards from the road to the Manse House but the drive was in need of some maintenance and it was littered with potholes that, in the dark, made it like a mine field. When Green hit the first deep pothole all three of them jumped and were shaken in their seats. Green stopped the car, thinking he might have gone into a ditch or hit something.

After a hissed discussion, they agreed it must be a pothole, and they backed out gingerly and tried to drive around it. Unfortunately, as he edged around to the left Green managed to put the driver's side front wheel into another larger cavity in the track. This time they went down with a thud. Sure, that they had damaged the wheel this time, they decided to get out and push the car out of the hole. They all suffered wet and muddy feet but didn't moan when they tripped in the dark. They were too close to their goal now to let anything get in the way. Using a torch, Evans picked his way up the lane to check the state of the rest of the road and confirm if they were at the right house or not. He came back with the news that they were in the right place and that the path was treacherous but they were at the right house. They decided to turn the car around so that nothing would impede their leaving when they were finished. Evans and Parson stayed outside the car and directed Green's turning as quietly as they could.

Back in the kitchen the fire had gone out, and Matt had woken up with a stiff neck and dead shoulder from having fallen asleep on the sofa. He shook Marieke gently. "Come on, we should go to bed," he whispered. It seemed so natural, she just nodded sleepily. Suddenly the spell was broken; he stood upright and still...listening, every nerve twitching. He couldn't hear it now, but something had caught his attention. He had thought he heard people talking outside. He shook his head. Now wouldn't be the time to start hallucinating again, he thought... they wouldn't come here... They'd go to mum's ... surely. Despite the logic, the paranoia had returned. He decided to check that the doors were locked and maybe take another quick peek down the drive.

Marieke was wide awake now. Wide eyed and pale, her heart pounded as she strained to catch whatever it was that he had heard. He laid his fingers gently across her lips, signalling for her to stay still and quiet as he silently walked through to the utility room and tentatively looked out the back door. It was dark and gloomy, how dull compared to our night on the hills, he thought. There was nothing to be seen. He pulled the door closed securing the latch and bolts. He thought about using his torch, but didn't want to attract attention from the neighbours.

Going through to the living room, he smiled at Kazik who was still sound asleep in his little nest on the couch. He walked over to the patio doors and moved just the corner of the curtain to give him a view out into the back garden. He still couldn't see anything, but he had an increasingly nagging feeling that they were not alone. Apart from a dog barking in the distance, the whole place seemed unnaturally still, as if the night itself was holding its breath waiting for something to happen. He closed the door gently, so as not to disturb the child. He headed down the hall to finally lock the front door. He had just reached the large doormat, a step away from the entrance and stretched out for the key, when suddenly the door burst open with a crash and the harsh glare of a flash light made him scrunch up his eyes in pain. He stepped forward, about to protest, thinking that it was a neighbour coming to investigate but stopped frozen in his tracks when he saw Parson, flanked by his henchmen, pointing a hand gun at him.

~~~
~~~

Chapter 19: Hard Evidence

Matt considered lunging at Parson's arm but he was too close; if the gun went off, even by accident, he would be in the way. Parson couldn't miss him at that range. Instead, he stepped back, his arms raised.

"Let's go meet the girlfriend shall we?" Parson smiled nastily as he moved forward into the house. Matt had no option but to turn and lead them into the kitchen.

Marieke pulled herself up onto the sofa, feet off the ground and pushing herself almost into the wall, she began to scream and shout hysterically in her native tongue. "Shut her up or I will," the gunman barked, pushing Matt towards her. "Find something to tie them up." Evans had come prepared, and he produced two rolls of thick brown tape. With one he bound Marieke shoving her roughly as he did so. With all the hate she could muster she spat in his face at close range. He slapped her hard in retaliation and bound the parcel tape around her mouth, head and hair, before pushing her back onto the seat. He threw the other roll to Green to secure Matt. Green was more cautious, not wanting to get too close, memories of their last encounter still fresh. But Matt did not resist, he was placid, almost helpful in holding out his wrists to be taped before being pushed back onto the sofa.

Evans found a tea towel and dried his face in disgust. He was muttering, not too quietly, "Dirty bitch."

"Enough!" interrupted his boss. He addressed the now pathetic looking couple, as tears fell silently down Marieke's face, which made him want to hit her himself. The lad looked defiant. I'll wipe that look off his arrogant mug too, thought Parson.

"You two have caused me far too much trouble. I hope you've had your fun, because no one messes with me and gets away with it!" His hate and loathing laced every word. In a zone of his own, knuckles white, holding the gun, little balls of spit formed in the corner of his mouth as he spoke. "So, where's this bloody evidence?"

There was no answer. Matt was the only one who could speak, as Marieke's mouth was taped, but he just sat there looking ahead, as if he hadn't heard. Parson viciously lashed out and kicked him sharply on the side of his knee. "I'm talking to you, shithead!" The ex-marine's eyes tightened slightly, but he made no other response.

"It's supposed to be in the nappy bag," Green reminded them. Matt remained staring blankly ahead but Marieke couldn't help herself; her eyes darted to the right, across the room to where they had dumped her meagre belongings. The glance was not lost on Evans who immediately rummaged through the bags and coats and produced a pastel coloured plastic bag that was zipped shut and bulged at the seams. He triumphantly placed it on the kitchen table with a thud. The three intruders smiled; finally, things were going their way.

"Would you like to do the honours?" Parson gestured to Green. The Brummy stepped forward and started to unpack nappies, baby wipes, creams, lotions and more nappies, now piled up on the table.

"What exactly d'you think we are looking for?" He looked at each of his colleagues feeling annoyed and foolish as nappies started to slide off the table onto the floor around his feet.

"Anything that ties us to that night and the nosey bint," suggested the Welshman.

"Could be her driving license, the samples she collected or the notes she made," snapped Parson. "Could be hidden in any of that," he waved his gun at the pile of baby paraphernalia on the table. "Can't you do anything, right? Look properly, you're supposed to be Police Officers for fuck's sake." The irony of this was not lost on Matt or Marieke as they exchanged glances. The two policemen got stuck in. They unfolded and even cut open the nappies; emptied tubs of cream and ripped open the packets of wipes, but found nothing that could be even vaguely considered as evidence. They were covered in creams and oils and beginning to get tetchy... it was all slipping away again.

Exasperated and now literally drooling with rage, Parson ripped the tape from Marieke's head. He shouted in her face prodding her hard as he spoke, spit bouncing off her skin. She cried, silently, but deeply; the sobs shuddering through her frail frame as he pushed her about like a rag doll.

It was Matt that broke. "For fuck's sake, she can't understand you," he growled.

Parson pulled himself up to his full height and turned slowly toward Matt. Looking down on him, he fiddled with the gun in his hand.

"But you do...I wonder if knee capping you would loosen your tongue?" He paused to see if the threat would work; he doubted it and shooting the lad at this point did not fit into his game plan. He had his alibi worked out, he knew what he had to do to walk away from all of this untouched and unfortunately that meant not torturing the Marine. Shame, he thought. Then he had a better idea.

"Where's the brat?" He brightened considerably. "Where is it? Malcolm, go find it. Let's see how much she understands when I start smashing his fingers... " He started to practise by hitting the butt of the gun into the palm of his left hand and laughing coldly.

Malcolm Green didn't move. Hurting children was something different, he was tired and fed up and beginning to think that there was no evidence. Perhaps it was just a ruse, thought up to threaten them. He never liked arguing with his boss, he was always brow beaten but there had to be another way. Looking at his feet, he started to mumble, "I'm not sure about this boss, we need to consider...." But he was interrupted by Parson's theatrical sigh.

"Look, we either get the evidence or kill the three of them and quite frankly, that might be the easiest option...either way you are as involved as I am and I hear they don't like coppers much in the Scrubs so get on with it."

Green was still not convinced. He shrugged his shoulders and stepping back raised his arms in supplication. Was Parson losing it? He needed to convince his boss to listen to him. "Wait a minute, I haven't killed anyone," he muttered.

Parson had had enough. He blamed Green for letting the girl escape in the first place. He would not stand for his insubordination too. Suddenly, a single shot rang out. Malcolm Green fell to the ground clutching his thigh, with blood oozing through his fingers.

"You bastard!" He gasped incredulously. He looked pleadingly at Evans, but the Welshman turned his head away and didn't move to help him.

Parson was almost whimsical.

"Sorry, didn't I mention the third scenario where you get shot in the cross fire? The gun comes from an unsolved shooting; I've now tied our squaddie here to that crime as well as assaulting you. I'll tell them how brave you were." He laughed, before his expression turned once more to ice. "We're wasting time - Evans, find the brat."

Evans nodded briefly and left the room, stepping over his colleague on his way. In the hall, he switched the light on, realising that he didn't know where the child was. It seemed logical to look in the bedrooms so he headed up the stairs. He had virtually searched the whole house before he finally made his way back down into the living room. He was frustrated and worried. Could they have hidden the kid with the evidence? This was becoming farcical. He didn't want to end up incurring Parson's wrath. Especially not while he was so wound up. Parson might turn the gun on him too.

He didn't see Kazik at first. There just seemed to be a pile of blankets on the couch. It was only when he turned the light on and crossed the room to investigate a noise coming from behind the curtain that he saw the child. A flood of relief ran through him, and for a second he dropped his guard and lost his concentration. Curious about the sound he had heard, as if somebody was rubbing at the window, he stepped over to the patio door and pulled back the curtain. Suddenly he was brought up short, shocked almost as much as Green had been when he was shot. He stared disbelievingly at the unsmiling face of Florence Macrury.

Florence scowled as she recognised Evans, shaking her head, her lips pursed. Colin

MacDonald, the young PC who had driven them the previous day, stood behind her, shining a torch over her shoulder. Evans was rooted to the spot and just stood gazing at them. The Inspector rapped on the glass impatiently, “Don’t just stand there, let me in!” She demanded.

Evans pretended to rattle the handle; he needed to buy himself some time. “Erm, I can’t. It’s locked. Come round the front, I’ll let you in.”

Florence was not convinced that she believed him. Having been alerted by the neighbours that there was something odd going on in a supposedly empty house, she had driven down expecting to evict a drunk or teenagers, not to meet up with her English opposite numbers in the middle of the night. She had hoped they had heeded her warning; she didn’t like the feel of this. What the hell were they doing here? Although she was sure he could have opened the door if he wanted, she decided that it would be quicker not to argue with him at this point.

She glared at him. “Just open the door you bloody tosser and let me in.” She barked at Evans. As she turned away, she told Colin to radio for reinforcements.

“Call in everyone on duty, I don’t trust *na dearg amadan,* these bloody idiots. We may be making more than one arrest.”

Evans glanced at the child. He was still asleep. He decided it would be best to leave him there. It might be of some sort of advantage if Parson didn’t know where he was. Heading back to the kitchen door, he called in a theatrically loud voice.

“Boss, Boss, it’s OK! Help is here. I’m just letting the Inspector in.”

Parson was momentarily confused. He was about to shout at Evans to get back and stop talking rubbish, when he heard the voices at the front door. His brain racing, he managed to change his demeanour as he saw the policewoman in the doorway. He grinned in mock relief and oozed.

“I am so pleased to see you Florence. We were going to call you for help but couldn’t get the phones to work. I have managed to disarm him though and Evans has secured them, unfortunately not before they shot Green in their attempt to escape.”

Florence didn’t answer; she tried to take in the scene quickly. Were Matt and that girl really tied up next to each other on the couch? She looked as bedraggled as he was belligerent. She couldn’t understand why nobody was helping the wounded Policeman on the floor. She stepped forward to the now semiconscious Green who was slumped in a growing pool of his own blood.

“Colin, get an Ambulance.... You...” turning to Parson, “Pass some of those nappies and cloths and I’ll try and stop the bleeding.” She wondered why there was a heap of baby products all over the floor, but that would have to wait.

Parson obeyed, but kept a firm grip on the gun, keeping it aimed at the bound pair on the couch.

Having done her best for Green, she turned her attention to Parson. He had a strange intensity about him that was somehow out of place. Matt, whom she'd known since he was a child, and the bedraggled looking girl, were looking at her intently. Matt was about to speak, but she narrowed her eyes and shook her head. To Parson, in a more casual voice she suggested, "Now that you've secured the situation, why don't you give me that gun, while we sort all this out?"

He didn't look at her, but kept his aim towards the couch.

"Are you armed? Or experienced in the use of fire arms? I think not. We are dealing with dangerous people here who you failed to do anything about. I think I'll stay in control thank you." His voice was pitched higher and his delivery was just that little bit quicker. Florence recognised him as a man on the edge.

Looking at Matt, she spoke to him quickly and quietly in Gaelic. "*Innse na- firinn gu du roin u seo? An do loisg thu an gunna*? Tell me the truth? Did you fire the gun?"

Matt replied, "*no, gu firinneach*! No – honestly!"

He was about to say more but Florence stopped him. She would get the full story later; just now he had confirmed her worst fear. She needed to disarm Parson.

"Thanks Nick," She smiled as she stood up. "I am trained alright, and this is my patch. It will make all the red tape a lot easier if I take over now, don't you think? Just give me the gun, and Colin and I will secure them into the car, and you can tell me everything that has happened." Although it stuck in her throat, she was reassuring and friendly. She needed him to believe she trusted him, to make him think she was on his side. "It will be easier with them out of the way and no more need for guns."

But it wasn't working. Parson just shook his head, without even glancing towards her. His tone was condescending and dismissive, as if he was talking to a truculent five year old.

"No, I'll tell you what's going to happen. Evans and I are going to get them into our car, and bring them back to the station. I would be grateful if you could attend to DC Green. Once I have them properly dealt with... that is, I mean, secured, I will give you a full statement. Ok?"

It wasn't really a question, and Florence wasn't used to being spoken to in such a manner and wasn't about to let it go. Moreover, she really did not want to leave the young people alone with this man. She needed to keep them all together.

"We'd be better using a Police car, they are equipped for prisoners. One of my guys will drive, you know that ..."

"No!" Blurted Parson fiercely. He turned, the gun now pointing towards Florence, his eyes were fierce. "Stop interfering, I've told you how it's going to happen, now just do as you are told." His hand was trembling, and his eyes were wide. "Evans, get over here and help me move the prisoners."

Up until this point, no one had been paying much attention to Matt and Marieke; they sat quietly, watching as the scene unfolded. This was exactly what Matt wanted, because it meant that nobody noticed what he was doing. When he allowed Green to bind him with the carpet tape earlier, he had banked that the policeman's inexperience in action would lead him into a schoolboy mistake; and it had. He'd hoped that Green wouldn't notice that his feet were angled slightly apart and his wrists were just a little bit twisted. Green had just thought that binding the boy's limbs at an angle would make him more uncomfortable, and less likely to be able to escape. What no one had noticed was that Matt, by slowly and gently moving his feet from heel to toe, and leaning his ankles outwards, bit by bit he was managing to loosen the ties around his legs. Working on his arms was more difficult, because he was sure that he would be noticed if he moved too much, but behind his back, he was tenaciously twisting his hands, to give himself more space. He was planning to be able to extract himself if and when they were put into the back or the boot of a car...which he thought was the most likely scenario. But when Parson beckoned Evans to join him, Matt had a better idea. He sat forward slightly and planted both feet firmly on the floor. He leaned forward slightly, moving his weight, ready to spring.

Neither policeman saw him as they were intent on each other. Like Green earlier, Evans was beginning to think that this had gone far enough, and that their best bet was to let the little policewoman take charge. After all, there's still no evidence, he thought....she'd seen him in the other room, he could claim he wasn't involved in the shooting and was trying to get out himself....rescuing the kid. Parson wasn't impressed by his hesitancy.

"Come on!" he snapped; waving the gun in the Welshman's direction. Shrugging his shoulders slightly and giving Florence a "Well, what else am I meant to do" look, he sidled slowly across the room. To reach Parson, he had to walk in front of the sofa. As he drew level with Matt, the Marine threw all his weight forward and with a roar sprung forward with all his might. He threw himself onto Evans, pushing them both across the room towards Parson at speed. Evans tried to push him off, but was caught off balance and could only go with the momentum, toppling onto his boss like a domino, praying that he wouldn't be shot.

Parson's slight frame was no match for the speed of the two bodies, and he was thrown to the ground in an undignified sprawl under his junior. He fired off a shot as he fell, but it only smashed into the plaster cornice above Florence's head. He lost his grip on the gun as his arm hit the fire surround and the gun careered across the floor into the pile of nappies. Florence leapt to the floor and retrieved it.

The two policemen groaned in shock. Matt was now in control. He rolled over on top of the two men, pulled himself up and sat firmly on top of Evans, who in turn was lying on his boss. They were both winded, but struggled to free themselves. With his hands still bound behind his back, Matt bounced with vigour once and then twice for good measure, and for the satisfaction of seeing them squirm in pain.

Florence quickly took charge, instructing PC MacDonald to cuff the two Met cops. She cut the bindings on Matt and Marieke, but instructed them to stay where they were, telling them that everyone would be taken back to the station until she got to the bottom of things.

As the cars arrived Marieke was panicking; she wanted to make sure that her son was safe. Matt told Colin where to find him, and the policeman headed out of the room. He had a moment of panic when all he could see was a nest of empty blankets on the sofa. He was about to raise the alarm, when he heard a shuffling noise to his left by the window. He looked over to see the dark curtain moving slightly. Stepping over, he lifted the curtain gently to reveal a pale tear stained face looking up at him. Poor bairn, he thought as he gently carried him out. Must have been terrified by the shooting.

Taking his mother's advice, Matt suggested that they call Father Ross to act as an interpreter. Florence had already had a complaint from one priest about a break in at his house, now she was going to have to explain the shooting. She wasn't convinced that she wanted to cope with waking two of them in the middle of the night.

Green was taken to hospital, and then later airlifted to the Southern General in Glasgow. The other two policemen, along with Matt and Marieke were installed in four of the five cells at the Police Station. Kazik was looked after by a local family, but was not allowed to take any of his own clothes or belongings. Florence wasn't sure why, but she was sure they were significant. PC Colin MacDonald was ordered to place the whole array of baby paraphernalia, strewn across the table and floor into evidence bags just in case. She was going to leave them all to stew overnight, while she caught up on the paperwork and informed all those who would want to fly in and take over in the morning.

Matt wouldn't wait. He continuously rang on his alarm bell in his cell. Eventually Florence relented and agreed to speak with him for five minutes. It was nearly dawn, and she'd had no sleep. She let Matt know in no uncertain terms that he'd better have something worthwhile to tell her. He told her where to find Marieke's statement in his rucksack which was still in the house, and to contact Iona and after some hesitation...Murdo MacNeil in

Glasgow. Florence sent the long suffering Colin back to Bornish to pick up the bag. Matt, his mind finally at rest, went to sleep. He was the only one who did that night.

~~~

Chapter 20: Visitors

Florence was busy with the paperwork for the rest of the night. She had only time for a quick shower and a bacon sandwich before she heard the reception bell ring, signifying that the mayhem was about to begin. She had read Marieke's statement over her breakfast and was still trying to come to terms with its content and impact, when Colin Macdonald interrupted her thoughts to tell her that Father Ross was waiting in reception to see her and more specifically to act as translator and, as he put it, "advocate" for the young girl. Florence instructed that he was to be shown to the meeting room and told that she would be with him shortly. She had been instructed to wait for CID officers from Inverness and some English officer and a Special Branch bigwig from Glasgow but she saw no harm in showing the priest the statement Matt had given her; after all it wasn't a Police document as such and if he could build a rapport with the girl and get more information from her that would save time when the mainlanders arrived. She was not convinced that she would be able to remain civil to the English gits, so had no problem leaving them to stew in their cells. As she got up to leave her office, the phone rang again. Colin reported that both Liz MacDonald and Sketch Macaulay had called, wanting to know on what grounds Matt was being held and when he was going to be released. Seonag Macaulay had rung too.

Florence smiled, "It hasn't taken the jungle drums very long: tell them that I am not saying a word till we get things sorted out, and if they pester me, they will be in a cell too, as possible accessories"...her tone then softened... "but tell Seonag I will call her later." Colin knew his boss well and understood. He paraphrased the messages to the callers. It was clear that the Inspector was not to be trifled with today.

Father Ross stood up as she entered the meeting room. He nodded his head in greeting as she waved that he should sit down again. She pulled over a chair as he began.

"I hope you don't mind my calling so early, it's just that after your message last night, I thought it best to get a prompt start. What can you tell me about all of this?"

He was a tall, neat man with short cropped hair, in his late forties. He was recognisable for
~~~

wearing his tweed flat cap and was known and respected in the community. Originally from Lewis, which was the northernmost island in the chain of islands that formed the Outer Hebrides, he was well travelled and enjoyed his reputation as a cosmopolitan, learned priest. Florence didn't think that she would shock him as she handed him the now crumpled looking sheets of paper.

"Have a read of that, while I get us a cup of coffee. I'll bring you up to date as to what has happened since they got here and then I'll tell you what I need to ask her."

Father Ross could sometimes be a stern character but when Florence returned to the meeting room, she could see the tell-tale start of a tear in the corner of his eye as he read. His long fingers shook slightly as he held the paper. On noticing her, he pulled himself together, blowing his nose with a large cotton handkerchief that he took from his pocket.

"I would like to see her as soon as possible," he said quietly.

"Yes," replied Florence and she went on to explain what they were going to do. Despite what she'd been told, she intended to speak to the girl and to Matt before her colleagues arrived from Inverness. She had called a woman PC in early in order that Marieke could be interviewed.

Marieke looked frail and terrified as she was led into the interview room. She was a slight figure; her eyes were red from crying and she constantly bit her bottom lip. She was picking at her fingernails as she stood beside the policewoman.

Like a terrified, anxious, bird, thought the priest. He smiled, trying to put her at ease. He introduced himself in Polish, because he was more confident speaking it than Romanian. He asked her if she spoke that language, to which she nodded slightly, and then told her that he was here to translate for her and to help if he could. As part of Florence's instructions, he offered her some breakfast.

She replied, speaking quickly and becoming animated and passionate. She still hadn't sat down. Pacing around the room, she was obviously highly distressed.

The Priest listened intently, nodded and said something, the tone of which sounded as if he was reassuring her. Turning to Florence he translated,

"She says that she will tell us whatever we want. She does not care if she goes to prison or is deported...but wants to know where her son is. She wants to see him and know that he is safe, and that Parson or his men cannot get to him."

Florence asked the priest to explain and reassure as best he could, that Kazik was safe, with a local family who were good people and would look after him as a police station was no place for a child. She also told him that Parson was being held securely in another cell, and would not be allowed near to her or her child. He did so.

Marieke shuddered at the concept that Parson was in the same building.

A senior woman police officer was a new notion to Marieke, but the fact that Florence was a woman, and although she hadn't really understood the conversation, she realised that the Inspector had not been fooled by Parson the previous night made her trust what the woman told her. She had been brought up to respect the clergy, and although this was not an Orthodox priest, she trusted his integrity as a man of God and felt calmed by his soft voice speaking in familiar words. She even gave a weak smile, when he switched to halting Romanian, after realising that it was her natural tongue.

The woman PC took notes, as they checked the statement Marieke had written for Matt and Kate, and they asked her about what had happened since she had arrived in Scotland. It took quite a while, but as they pieced together her story, they were amazed by her determination and couldn't help but believe that what she had told them was the truth.

Marieke finally signed her statement. Looking up at the clock, Florence realised that there was only about forty-five minutes until the Glasgow plane came in.

"Let's stop here for a moment," she suggested. "To give you a rest and some breakfast as we promised." She waited while this was translated. "I want to speak with young Matt, before our visitors arrive," she explained to the priest.

"Can I stay with Marieke?" He asked.

"I don't see why not, I can trust you not to do a runner, can't I?" She smiled.

She had just settled into the second interview room with Matt when she heard the reception buzzer ring again.

"We're going to run out of space," she muttered. There was a knock on the door. That was quick, she thought as Colin came in. "Who's in reception now?" She asked, ready to send them off with a flea in their ear; she didn't have time for local busybodies today.

Colin seemed confused by the question. "Er, I dunno, a man. I'll see to him; you have to come now. You have a very important phone call."

"For God's sake Colin," she sighed. "I'm busy, can't you take a message?"

The young police constable shook his head solemnly. Florence thought that he looked oddly "star struck". "Who is it that's so important then?" She was trying hard to keep the sarcasm out of her voice. Colin looked at Matt then back at Florence. He was nervously hopping from one foot to another, holding onto the door.

"Well? Spit it out."

"It's the Chief Constable, ma'am, and he wants to speak to you now," he blurted. There was a pause, while the Inspector digested this information. She had not met or spoken to the Chief before. It was a rare occurrence for him to ring Police Stations early on a Friday morning let alone one in the Outer Hebrides.

"He's on the office phone?" She asked. Colin nodded. "Ok, you stay here with Matt and I'll take it in there, that'll be quickest. Your man in reception will have to wait."

Florence unconsciously brushed down the front of her uniform and straightened her hair as she went to take the call. She even stood to attention as she greeted the most senior Police Officer in Scotland. The Chief Constable also seemed to be having a busy morning, as he was brief and to the point. He told her that he had sent a gentleman by the name of Murdo MacNeil, to sort out the "Parson business". He didn't give MacNeil's rank or title, just said that he was, "associated with Special Branch" and she was to, "offer him every courtesy and co-operation". Florence had barely confirmed that she would, when he thanked her and hung up. Still standing, she replaced the handset. The buzzer in reception sounded again. She was about to send Colin, then hesitated. She thought it was highly unlikely, but just on the off chance...she had better go herself.

A tall, nicely tanned man in a dark suit, with big brown eyes smiled at Florence and held out his hand. "Hi, I'm Murdo MacNeil, hopefully somebody has told you to expect me?" As he held her hand, his eyes twinkled. She felt the colour rise in her cheeks. Behave yourself woman, he's just a Weegie Copper.

"Hmm, yes, but I wasn't expecting you here quite this soon. The Glasgow flight isn't in yet, is it?"

"Suppose not, I caught the early flight via Stornoway. Wanted to beat the rush. Any chance we can see young Mr. Macaulay?"

"Yes of course," bustled Florence. "Follow me, please." She led him through reception to the interview room where Matt was sitting with Colin drinking a cup of coffee.

"Och laddie, you've had quite a week, haven't you?"

"Aye, you could've warned me they were complete nutters though."

"I didnae ken, I'm sorry." Murdo sat down. His smooth facade slipped for a moment, he looked worried. "Are you all right?" Florence pulled up a chair beside him. She was surprised at the exchange; it hadn't occurred to her that they might know each other.

"Yeah," grinned Matt. "Have you seen Iona and Kate?"

"Aye, last night. Got DNA from the sample, so just a matter of identifying it."

Florence was now totally confused, and beginning to feel annoyed that they weren't including her.

"Would either of you gentlemen like to explain what's going on?" She was sitting up straight, her eyebrows above the line of her fringe. Matt smiled, he remembered that look from when he'd been a cheeky schoolboy and she was the local Poileas.

MacNeil explained the favour that he had asked of Matt earlier that week. "We'd been watching Evans and Green but didn't know who was running the show. It had to be someone senior for them to get away with it for so long. There are more of them, though. One of his cronies came up to Glasgow to try and squash Marieke's account and bury it." He paused, thinking for a moment. "She did have evidence though, and Matt here, had the brain wave of getting it to me with his sister when she was airlifted out to the maternity unit. Kate called me; you should have seen your mother's face when I walked in!" He smiled, "but Kate gave me the bag, with the samples. I got it to the lab, and well, here we are. I just need a DNA sample from Parson, to put him at the scene." He stretched his arms and looked around. "We don't have much time though. I think one of his cronies is on the flight from Glasgow." He leant towards Florence.

"I need to get Marieke and the boy away to a place of safety. Where are the Met at the moment? Have you charged them yet?"

"In the cells, and no," she replied," I was told to wait for CID from Inverness."

"When will they get here?"

"They're coming on the ferry." She looked at her watch," They'll be here in about an hour."

"After the plane?"

"Just," Florence confirmed.

MacNeil paused for thought again.

"I really think you should charge them. The sooner the better, doesn't matter what for." He shrugged. "Let's just make sure they are formally tied into Scottish Jurisdiction before anyone gets off that plane. It will make it harder for anybody to spirit them away, eh?"

Florence didn't need any further encouragement. It would make her day to nail that arrogant blaigeard, and having it all sorted out by the time the Inverness crew turned up, with the Chief Constable's blessing, would just be the icing on the cake. She couldn't help but grin.

As Florence prepared to formally charge her remaining prisoners, Murdo rose to talk with Marieke. "What should I do? Can I see Marieke before you go?" asked Matt.

"Hmm...I need to get her out of here... they're a dangerous bunch, I dinnae want any of Parson's cronies even knowing what she looks like. You need to make a formal statement here... but go home first, then come and see me in Glasgow in a couple of weeks." He turned to go, then turned back and shook Matt's hand. "Thank you. I really mean it... Oh, by the way, you need to ring your family. You're an uncle now ye ken!" He waved as he left the room, leaving Matt standing open mouthed.

Inspector Macrury prided herself on running a tight efficient ship. But that morning, even they managed to step up a gear. Papers were prepared and the two policemen, while totally astonished, were charged in their cells. With help from Father Ross, Murdo explained to Marieke that he was taking her back to Glasgow, to keep her safe, until Parson was properly behind bars. She was concerned at the thought of being separated from Matt. He was one of the few people in her short life whom she had been able to trust, who had made her laugh and made she and Kazik feel safe. She didn't want to lose him. MacNeil promised that they would be able to meet up again, realising it would probably be easier to let them have a brief goodbye, if only to reassure her to cooperate.

The challenge was how to spirit the woman and child off the island quickly, without being seen and without the complication of any identification papers for either of them. Florence demonstrated the benefit of her local knowledge and influence by blagging them a lift on an army helicopter from the Rocket Range to the Kyle of Lochalsh, where Murdo could get them picked up. She also managed to buy them a little extra time by ensuring that one of Sketch's Taxis picked the Met policeman up from the airport, and brought him to the station via the "scenic route".

"But it's a three minute drive?" questioned the driver.

"Not if you go via East Camp and Market Stance..." she replied.

This allowed the Inverness CID Team to arrive first. They were initially slightly put out at being told to work to the local Inspector's command but when they realised how high a level that order came from, they toed the line, and didn't ask too many questions about simply escorting two prisoners back to Glasgow.

When Superintendent John Bird eventually arrived, he was charming, gracious and full of compliments about the islands and the efficiency of the local force in what he referred to as "apprehending dangerous individuals". Inspector Macrury agreed, knowing full well that they were not referring to the same "dangerous individuals".

She wasn't fooled. She thought that Bird was an apt name. He had a large protruding chin, which reminded her of the bill of some exotic bird she had once seen in a zoo. He was tall with a protruding pot belly. "Like a pregnant stork," thought Florence. They had done the pleasantries; she was momentarily lost in her own thoughts and didn't hear his question. He cleared his throat a little dramatically.

"Oh sorry, I've been up all night...did you say something?" She was annoyed with herself.

He smiled reassuringly. "Oh, I do understand, believe me," he gushed. "Perhaps I can be of help? Maybe I could interview the prisoners for you?"

Florence smiled inwardly; she'd been waiting for this. "No thank you, that's very good of you, but I've interviewed two, and the other two are going to Glasgow to be questioned there."

"Ah, I see." He replied, although the way he shifted in his seat and looked around the room made it obvious that he didn't see at all.

"Sometimes," he ventured, "there's an advantage in having a second chat...You know, by someone who's not so closely involved..... How about I have a chat with this Matt or the girl... get to the bottom of it, eh?"

"That won't be necessary, thank you." Florence answered flatly. She was wide awake now and watching his every move.

"Can I interview them? It will help me understand and clear up the actions of my officers."

"No."

"I beg your pardon?" Bird was obviously not used to being denied by a junior officer.

"I'm not trying to be unhelpful," smiled Florence. "It's just that the translator has gone, so you won't be able to speak with the girl and well, we let Mr. Macaulay go about half an hour ago." She shrugged her shoulders and smiled. Bird stood up and started walking around the room, shaking his head in utter disbelief. "Do your superior officers know about this?" He was looking at her as if she had grown a second head... or just admitted to dealing drugs or worse.

"Oh yes," smiled Florence. "They are fully aware of his part in the whole episode." She was quite pleased that she was managing to tell the truth, without mentioning that Marieke had left about half an hour previously after a tearful goodbye with her protector of the previous week. She had sent Matt home to get some rest, to return later, to make a full statement once, "All the fuss had died down" as Murdo had put it.

Bird was obviously perplexed. Things were not as he had expected to find them and he was not getting the cooperation he had anticipated and felt that he deserved.

"Can I see Inspector Parson then?" His tone had lost its veneer, and was somewhat terser.

"Why yes, of course. I will arrange for you to use an interview room." She went to pick up the phone.

Bird felt he had regained at least a little traction. "I'll see if I can make arrangements to escort them back to the mainland for you."

Florence smiled again. In fact, she was having trouble keeping a straight face. "No need, thank you, that's all right. My colleagues from Inverness are here to do that... Let me get that room set up for you."

This time, she left the room and instructed Colin MacDonald to fetch Parson from his cell. She regretted that she didn't have a two way mirror in the interview room but suspected that she knew what they would be talking about.

With Bird out of the way, Florence took the opportunity to brief her colleagues in the operations room. They discussed what had taken place and the logistics of removing the Met officers back to Glasgow. They had just agreed a plan and were recharging their coffee cups, when Bird strode into the room. He studiously avoided looking at or addressing Florence. Turning to the men in the room, he asked if the visiting officers from Inverness were present. Inspector Donnie MacDougall, Florence's opposite number; a well built balding man in his forties, with a broad Aberdonian accent, identified himself. Bird sat down opposite him. Looking very solemn and self important, he shook his head and asked quietly to be put in contact with the regional superior at head office. As soon as possible.

MacDougall didn't like the tone of the man's voice, nor his obvious discourtesy to Florence. He knew she could be a pain, but it was her station after all.

"What's the problem?" was his curt response.

Bird met his eye with a supercilious glare. "Never in my twenty two years on the force, working throughout the UK, have I ever come across such a botched up, mishandling of what should have been the simple arrest of two wanted felons. Obviously fuelled by a narrow minded parochial approach, coupled with downright incompetence, these police officers have been charged with kidnap and attempted murder... while the felons have either disappeared or been set free... ridiculous, to say the very least." He cleared his throat and sat straighter as he continued. "As senior officer here, I intend to remedy this and see if we can apply some damage limitation. I will get the clearance to take charge from the regional HQ but in the meantime, we need to re-arrest..."

"Thank you for your concern," interrupted MacDougall, "but you have no authority here, while I am the Senior Scottish Officer. I have been instructed, from the highest level, that Inspector Macrury is the Officer in Command today and as far as I can see she has everything in hand. There are no outstanding warrants for either Mr Macaulay or Miss Manover. In fact, one of them, I believe, was working for Glasgow Special Branch." MacDougall threw that snippet of information in to gauge the Englishman's reaction and got an immediate result. Bird's face blanched and he physically shuddered.

Florence leant forward to twist the knife. "Parochial and incompetent I may be, but you are forgetting that I and my officers were there...we saw who was tied up; who was holding the gun and who was bleeding. Not what I would call a straight forward arrest, even in my obviously limited career." Furious, she hardly trusted herself to say any more. "Now if you will excuse us, we have work to do... Colin, can you escort this gentleman out... no, we should be more courteous, escort him back to the airport, so that he can arrange his flight home."

At that the OIC left the briefing room, signalling for MacDougall to join her. Neither acknowledged Bird as they left, who, stunned by this treatment, sat looking bewilderedly at the desk. He didn't have Parson's confidence or arrogance. Florence wondered how he had got mixed up in this sordid saga and what it was that he had to hide.

~~~
~~~

Chapter 21: Family

It was about ten thirty in the morning when Matt Macaulay stepped out of Benbecula Police Station. His eyes squinted at the brightness of the spring sunshine. He rolled his shoulders, glad of the warmth, after his night sleeping in the cells. He was mightily relieved that they had managed to get Parson and his men behind bars but felt strangely alone without Marieke and her son. He tried to brush that thought away. He'd only known her a few days after all, but it had been an eventful few days. He smiled to himself but his thoughts darkened. Had he done the right thing letting her go with Murdo? Could he be trusted? His reverie was broken by the loud blast of a car horn. He looked over the street towards the military camp, there was a familiar car parked in the lay-by. Sketch leaned over and opened his passenger door. "Get in Laddie, needin a lift are ye? I'll take you to your auntie Liz's."

Matt didn't argue, and was very soon sitting in his aunt's kitchen telling her and his cousin Sketch about his adventures of the last few days. They were suitably impressed. Amazed at what they were hearing, they were pleased that despite the ordeal he was describing, they hadn't seen Matt this animated and positive in months. They were relieved on more than one level. Liz thought about how happy her sister would be, and then thought again.

"Matt, what am I thinking. You'd better ring your mam...she has news for you too."

"Aye, Iona's had the baby, hasn't she? What happened? Is she ok?" he remembered Murdo's throw away comment.

"Ring your mother..." smiled Liz. "She'll want to tell you herself."

Matt refilled his mug of tea from the pot on the stove and went out to the back step to phone his mum. His excuse was that he would get better phone signal there, but he also wanted a little more privacy to discuss all that had happened to him and his night in a police cell. The sun felt warm on his back as he selected her number. He felt like a small boy as he experienced reassuring warmth at the sound of his mother's voice. Once he confirmed that he was safe and well and not been arrested for anything, she was reassured too. He promised that he would explain the full story in person.

She accepted this but asked simply, "Is everything sorted with that girl and the wee bairn? Are they safe now?"

Good question, he thought. He hoped so, but decided to change the subject. "I believe I am an uncle...but I don't know what to?" Still in Glasgow, Seonag didn't need any more problems. She told Matt how Iona's condition had deteriorated in Southern General. Not only was her blood pressure high, but there were signs of the baby becoming distressed so there was no option but to give her an emergency caesarean. Luckily, her husband Iain was in time to be with her, leaving Iona to sit and wait, "me saying my prayers", until Kate turned up.

"With that Murdo MacNeil. I didn't know what was going on; she started rummaging through her sister's things and then gave Murdo the nappy bag! She kept saying it was for you...but didn't explain properly until afterwards. He didn't hang about, mumbled something about getting to the lab and left. That's when Iain came back to tell us he was a dad to a wee boy. He is very wee. Only four pounds two ounces, so they are keeping him in the Special Care Unit for a couple of days to keep an eye on him. Benjamin James... tiny, but still handsome."

"How's Iona?" Matt Interrupted.

"Well they have her on a drip and resting. They say she is out of danger and improving, but she looks very frail and drained. She'll rest now that Iain's here and the baby's OK. She knew about the nappy bag too and asked if Murdo picked it up. You'll have to tell me what it was I was smuggling."

"My mam...international smuggler without even knowing it!" he laughed. "Honestly I'll tell you when I understand it all myself."

They discussed the family's travel plans. Seonag was going to stay a couple of days with her daughter but Iona and Ben would be travelling home with Iain once they were well enough and Iain had sorted out his new car. Matt felt a pang of guilt, partly for Iain but more so for Kate as he remembered that her car was still parked at Uig pier. He explained that he was giving a statement to the Police later on but expected to have to meet up with Murdo in Glasgow over the next couple of days, so would be able to help out if needed.

After the call, Sketch drove Matt home so that he could have a shower and get changed before he returned to Balivanich to give his statement. Knowing that everyone was safe and well, as far as they could be, he felt relaxed. Although tired, he had no ill effects from the previous night's ordeal. In fact, he felt quite exhilarated; pleased at a job well done and happy to have contributed to neutralising some seriously nasty pond scum as he saw it. Just like the old days, he thought. Then there was Marieke. He wasn't sure how he felt about her. After all he had only known her for less than a week but it was a very intense week that had thrown them close together. He admired her spirit and determination. He liked the way her eyes twinkled when she finally smiled and he remembered how she smelt of flowers and was so soft and small when she cuddled into his chest. Like a little rag doll.

"Snap out of it," he chastised himself. But then he remembered Kazik's wide eyed awe at the sight of the sea and his lopsided grin as he played, obviously enjoying feeling safe and free. "Oh shit," he muttered. Before being ill, Matt had the reputation of being a "bit of a tart". He enjoyed being young free and single. With his quirky looks, he never had any trouble chatting up young women but had never been enticed to settle down. It was a new feeling to him as he slowly realised that this young woman meant something...he didn't know what but definitely "something" to him. He would have to see them again.

Matt arrived back at the police station just before two. He was expecting to sit down and talk things through with Florence. He'd known her since he was a child and had no inhibitions about telling her the whole story.

But it wasn't Florence who came into the small reception area to meet him. A tall balding man, in a crumpled suit held out his hand. Only offering the briefest of smiles, he introduced himself as Detective Inspector Donnie MacDougall, from Inverness. He spoke with an East Coast drawl as he explained that he would be taking Matt's statement to ensure independence. Matt was slightly surprised and not sure of the implications of what was being said. This doubt must have shown on his face as MacDougall hesitated, "You don't have a problem with that, do you?" His voice had acquired a harder edge.

"No, not at all, let's just get on with it." Matt sighed, he suddenly felt very tired. He knew he had nothing to hide but he did not know how much influence Murdo MacNeil really had or how his own actions would appear under the cold scrutiny of Scottish legal bureaucracy.

The discussion regarding who would obtain Matt's statement had taken place after John Bird had left the Station. Florence understood that the case against the Met officers had to be watertight. She did not want to be accused of any collusion with Matt over his evidence, as they were both witnesses to the events in the old Manse. MacDougall agreed with her. He hadn't liked Bird's attitude and the fact that he had tried to pull rank as he had but he couldn't help but wonder if he had a point about how Florence had handled the arrests. Had she just let a potential illegal immigrant disappear with this man from Glasgow? He didn't know who this MacNeil guy was. He wasn't a proper policeman; whereas Parson, Evans and Green were, and from what he could see, appeared to be respected officers. Moreover, Florence seemed to be condoning the irrational actions of this ex-Marine, who'd been considered unfit by the Services after all. He'd always felt that she could be a bit of a maverick. He didn't know how she'd obtained the "Top Cover" that she was enjoying that morning, however he had to ensure that she didn't make a fool of the Scottish Constabulary in what could be a very high profile dispute between the English and Scottish Police.

It turned out to be a very long afternoon. It wasn't that MacDougall was rude or aggressive but to Matt's mind he just didn't get it. He listened without comment to the whole story. They went back over the various incidents over and over again. He couldn't understand why Matt hadn't just dialled 999 when he saw Marieke being attacked. Or if he had seen Murdo MacNeil's credentials before he left the station with the woman. Murdo had asked him to stay around Glasgow, but he didn't do that. Did he have his own agenda? The conversation went on to examine why he hadn't just dialled 999 in Fort William or in Benbecula rather than go to such elaborate efforts to disguise themselves and hide in obscure places. Matt tried to explain that it was because Parson, who was after all the poileas, had twisted the facts so much in Glasgow and that Murdo had been vague about his role, that Matt didn't trust the authorities. This seemed an alien concept to MacDougall. Matt patiently explained that it was only after he read Marieke's statement that he decided that extreme measures were needed to cope with an extreme situation. He defended his actions on the grounds that he had seen the violence Evans and Green were capable of, so he wanted to keep Marieke and Kazik safe until the evidence could be dealt with by the experts. They intended to hand themselves into Florence once they knew the bag was in Glasgow but Parson somehow beat them to it.

MacDougall obviously did not know the nature or the importance of the evidence. Matt decided not to elaborate. His patience was wearing thin. He was fed up with helping the Poileas now and tired of not being believed by people who didn't have the whole story. He decided that MacDougall was going to have to work it out for himself.

They were going round in circles and beginning to become fractious when MacDougall decided that he'd had enough. At 10.30pm he terminated the interview, telling Matt not to leave the Island as they would probably want to speak with him again and if his story could not be verified, possibly charge him with at least perverting the course of justice. Neither impressed nor surprised, Matt simply asked MacDougall if he could go. When the policeman finally agreed, Matt shrugged on his jacket and headed out of the station. He waved goodnight to a bemused looking PC at the desk but didn't glance back as he got into his car.

He took a few moments to pull himself together before he drove off. He wondered if they were watching him from the window. He wasn't too worried by MacDougall but annoyed that he had been treated like a criminal again, when others in the force, including Florence who was probably just in another room, knew that he wasn't at fault. He wondered if Marieke was being treated the same way. It wasn't right.

Looking at his watch again, he considered going to the pub for "Last Orders", he could do with a drink... but everyone would want to know about what had gone on, each with their own pet theories...The rumour mill will have been running rife. He was too tired to face all that.

~~~
~~~

Chapter 22: Loose Ends

The next few days were frustratingly quiet. Matt rattled around the house. With Seonag and Iona away, he missed the usual hustle and bustle of his family and the warmth and chemistry that had grown between himself and Marieke. His heart wasn't in the everyday chores of the croft. He'd rung the police station several times but had been told politely but firmly that they would contact him if further information or action was required. He'd only managed to have a brief conversation with Kate. She'd headed south following a lead about further misinformation in the "Better Together" Campaign. His mother, although not usually a gushing person, was simply full of her new grandson. He was pleased to hear that his sister was steadily getting better but found it hard to relate to a child he hadn't met yet. Infuriatingly, Murdo was not answering his phone. It didn't even go to voicemail, so he couldn't even leave a message. Not knowing what was going on was driving him mad and the fact that he couldn't even get on the plane to go and find out was also winding him up.

"What are they going to do? Arrest me for trying to visit a Police Station?" He moaned to Callum. But that was part of the problem; would he go to a Police Station? He wasn't even sure where he would find Murdo.

Finally, his family came home but the joy of the baby, although he shared it, heightened his sense of loss. Not only was he anxious about the case, he was really worried about Marieke and Kazik. He decided he had to go to Glasgow. He had taken to dialling Murdo's number randomly, whenever he had a spare moment although he'd stopped expecting a response. Because of this he was taken a little by surprise when, on answering his phone, a Glaswegian voice greeted him

"Hello Matt, how ya doing? I hear you have been trying to get hold of me."

They arranged to meet in Glasgow the following Friday. Murdo said that he would clear it with the local police. Matt asked if he would be able to meet up with Marieke while he was there but Murdo became somewhat evasive at that point. Suggesting that "he would see what was possible." Matt didn't see what the problem was but decided he would have that discussion face to face.

This time he flew to the City. The family joked that it would be a long time before any of them would lend him a car again. He took the morning flight arriving in Glasgow just before lunchtime.

He and Murdo had agreed to meet in the bar of the Holiday Inn opposite the airport. It was only a short walk, dodging tourists with wheelie bags along the front of the airport to the hotel. Matt made his way into the large entrance hall. The bar was at the end of an open area to the left, with mirrors, armchairs and sofas scattered around. Matt positioned himself so that he could see the bar and the lobby, ready for Murdo's arrival.

He was late. Matt had got through several cups of coffee and a BLT before he arrived. Eating his sandwich, he had watched the ebb and flow of people going back and forth through reception. Some were obviously on holiday. Others looked nervous about an imminent flight. He smiled at what looked like a couple on an illicit rendezvous. There were men hanging around just as he was. He made a silent note of them, wondering if he was being watched and if so, by whom.

Matt watched Murdo arrive. He was in no rush. Stopping for a moment at reception, making a short phone call, before he eventually turned and scanned the lounge, nodding slightly in recognition of the Uibhistach before he made his way over. Matt was not surprised but felt a pang of disappointment that Marieke and Kazik were not with him.

Murdo enquired about Matt's flight but the young man wanted to get straight to the point. He wanted an explanation for the last ten days and he needed to know that Marieke and her son were safe. Murdo nodded.

"That's why I was late," he explained. "We have them in a very safe location. I have an agreement in principle that you can visit but needed to arrange your transport. We don't want you to be followed and you'll have to agree to certain conditions."

He looked around the bar and moved slightly forward. Was he looking for watchers too? He was going to give Matt the impression that he was doing him a favour, but actually the girl kept asking for him, so he and his employers felt it would help all round to allow them to spend some time together.

"What conditions?" Matt asked warily.

"With Parson and Evans behind bars and Green under guard in hospital, we think we've dealt the gang a major blow but we can't underestimate his influence. They are still in danger and their location must remain secret. We're also not that keen on anyone knowing the location of our safe houses." He raised his eyebrows to emphasise the point. "So, this is what is going to happen. I have told that wee lassie at reception that you are Mr. Macdonald. You have a room booked here, 214." He handed Matt a key card. "In a little while someone will ask for you. They will know your room number. They will drive you to the destination."

He paused; Matt suspected that he was going to like the next bit even less. "When you get close to the destination, you will be asked to put a hood over your head and keep it on until you are inside the house. You can stay as long as you like today. But leave the same way. Return here and we will meet up again tomorrow." Matt didn't respond immediately. He instinctively glanced around the room again, almost without moving his head.

"Bit cloak and dagger... why can't we just...?"

"Take it or leave it," Murdo interrupted. "We can't have it any other way...you've seen what they are capable of."

Matt couldn't disagree with that but he was still not content. "But that's the other thing. I know you're not the Poileas...you need to explain who "we" are and why I should trust you."

"I'll explain all that tomorrow. The window to see her is today, no budget for coppers on overtime to ferry you around at the weekend." He smirked, it was Matt's turn to raise his eyebrows. "No, I'm keeping this tight, very few know you'll be visiting. It's with today's shift or not at all.... and as for trust..." he sighed and looked up holding eye contact with the younger man. "It's been me trusting you so far... twice I think. First on that hillside... and then when I gave them into your custody."

"You didnae tell me what I was in for," snapped Matt.

"You didnae do as you were told," retorted Murdo.

They sat in silence. A waitress approached offering further refreshments. Murdo ordered an Espresso, Matt decided on a large Malt. He reckoned, he might need a bit of something to help him through the afternoon. He mulled everything over in his mind. He didn't like not being in control...that's why he hadn't done as he was told, and that's why he felt uneasy now but he could understand the logic of what Murdo was saying. "Ok," he finally agreed, "But?"

"Don't worry about the buts son. We can talk through all that tomorrow. Nine o'clock here?" Murdo didn't wait for a response. He finished his coffee and stood up. There was the slightest hint of a smile as he turned and left the lounge bar.

Matt watched his back as he left. Nobody appeared overly interested or followed him. He could see him through the large windows heading along the path back towards the airport. He wasn't going to the car park, so he didn't drive here, he watched him cross the road. Heading for an airport Taxi, nice and anonymous. Matt mused. God, I'm thinking like him now! He sat back to wait for his driver.

It was another forty minutes before a slight, nondescript man in jeans and a denim jacket strolled into the bar. He had tatty attire, but a smart hair cut and office hands. Oh shit, thought Matt. If we are being watched, he's as obvious as PC Plod and he's the one Murdo trusts!

He came over. "Mr. MacDonald, room 214?"

"Aye."

"Your car's outside sir."

Matt followed him out of the hotel, at a slight distance. Nobody seemed to be interested in them, either in the lobby, the car park as he got into the back seat of the vehicle, or as they pulled onto the M8 into the city.

The traffic was slow, but they didn't stay on the motorway for long. PC Plod seemed to be taking every back street and rat run in the city. Matt wondered if he was doing this to confuse him or shake any potential company. Nonetheless he had a vague idea where he was. He wanted to keep track...just in case. It was shortly afterwards that PC Plod spoke again, but he wasn't making conversation. "Mr. Macdonald, on the floor beside you is a small bag. Inside you will find a black hood, which you are expecting. Please place it over your head and pull the draw string, and then lower yourself in your seat, so as not to attract attention." Matt removed the hood from the bag. It was like an old fashioned sports bag, made of a thick black material, with a cord to pull it tight. Even the thought of putting it on made him feel vulnerable. He stretched at the material, examining the draw string. He'd keep hold of that. The driver half turned towards him, "ehm, you need to be putting it on in the next couple of minutes or we'll be turning back to the airport." Matt slowly pulled the hood on. It had no smell and a fleece like feel. He had already worked through potential scenarios in his head. He was safe enough while they were moving. It was when the car stopped that he would keep a tight hold of the draw string and his wits about him.

Matt calculated that they must have driven for a further ten minutes. He tried to keep track of the number of turns they were making and the general sense of direction they were travelling in. He had a feeling that they were heading into the suburbs on the west of the city but he couldn't be sure. Finally they slowed right down and pulled left into a gravel drive. Plod manoeuvred the car and stopped.

He spoke again. "I'm going to open up then come round and open your car door. Take two or three steps straight out of the car and you will come to the front door. Go in, close it behind you, then take the hood off. Ok?" Matt was thinking. "Ok?" Plod repeated. "There's no need for anything silly, we're on the same team. This is a routine precaution."

"Maybe routine in your world pal," responded Matt. "Let's just get on with it." He listened to his every move as the other man walked around the vehicle. His heart was pounding as the door opened and he felt his way out. After two tentative steps, he felt the edge of a door step under his foot. Keeping hold of the draw string with one hand he reached forward with the other. He felt the door and as promised it pushed open. As he stepped inside the door was pulled shut behind him. He removed the hood.

He didn't see the figure that rushed towards him, just a blur of a person as his eyes readjusted to the light but before he knew it Marieke had thrown her arms around his neck and her legs around his waist. Hugging him, laughing and crying at the same time. He held her tight, as she snuggled into his neck. Her hair was soft against his face.

"Hello to you too," he whispered. She turned her face upwards, brushing her lips against his cheek. Neither was capable of turning away, both felt the spark which had been suppressed for so long burst into a flood of emotion as they held each other close. Part of Marieke wanted to kiss him deeply and warmly, she wasn't ready but she now was sure it would come. She was feeling human again. Matt understood and didn't push her. He didn't know if they were alone, he didn't care. He was where he needed to be. The spell was broken as Matt became aware of an odd feeling on his leg. Something was pulling at his trousers. He looked down and started to laugh. There was Kazik, pulling on his jeans, holding his arms up and jumping from one foot to another. He wanted to be included in the welcome too. Matt gently let Marieke slide her legs to the floor, still holding her around the waist and picked the little boy up with his other arm. They all stood for a minute feeling reassured and relieved in each other's presence and safety. Eventually Marieke gestured that they go on into the house. She went ahead as Kazik took his hand to lead him in. They walked down a short hall. To the right a staircase was visible to its first landing, a kitchen was straight ahead, Matt thought he glimpsed a figure moving behind the half open door. Marieke opened a door to the left leading into a living room. Matt didn't follow immediately.

"Hello!" This time he spoke loudly and pointedly. Another woman appeared in the kitchen doorway. "I'm Matt..."

"I know," She interrupted.

"And you are?" he continued.

"Protection duty sir. She doesn't speak much English. Do you want help with translation?"

"No, I think we'll manage," replied Matt. "Wouldn't mind a cup of tea though." He decided it would be best to keep her busy.

He followed Marieke into the living room. It was clean but sparsely furnished. It reminded him of services accommodation. It was neat and adequate but somehow lacking soul or comfort. The walls were magnolia. With one cheap looking print of somebody's dogs hung crookedly on the wall. There were large patio doors which led into a garden, but they were screened by a full length opaque white blind, which made the room seem gloomy despite the bright afternoon. There was a three piece suite with a polyester cover of faded flowers, which looked like it had seen better days. Marieke seemed content enough with it. He asked if Kazik was able to play in the garden.

She shook her head, "They want nobody to see us," She explained. "But he likes that." She pointed at a television in the corner that was switched onto a children's programme. "Pig!!" Kazik pointed at the cartoon. Matt chuckled. "So, he's learning English?" They both laughed and nodded.

"I speak more too," boasted Marieke

"So, we don't need this?" Matt held up his Smart phone.

"It will help," smiled Marieke, taking it out of his hand.

All three of them settled down together on the couch. Kazik was mainly watching the cartoon, while Matt and Marieke used the phone to catch up on what had happened since they had parted. The policewoman joked when she brought in the tea, that he should make Marieke practise her English. Aye, Matt thought, and you'd be listening in. The translation device gave them at least some degree of privacy.

Using the translator app and talking quietly, Matt established that Marieke had been treated OK. She looked well; she'd lost the terrified haunted look. She had been given a letter by Murdo, which she showed to him. There were two copies, one in English and the other in Romanian. In return for her testimony, she and her son would be given safe custody and protection until the trial. Afterwards, if she wished to remain in the United Kingdom, her application for a visa would be considered favourably.

Matt didn't think it was that good an offer, but she seemed pleased with it. "I made them write it", she explained. "I want to live in Scotland. I like the ..." she used her arms to illustrate "...big... land...up?"

"Mountains?" Suggested Matt. To which she nodded.

Taking note of what she said, he tried to explain that the letter wasn't a guarantee. She looked perplexed. "Murdo said it would be OK," she insisted. "We need bad men in prison. We are safe now. Have ..." she thought for a moment "future?" Matt nodded that she had the right word. "It was like a very bad sleep."

"Nightmare," Matt suggested.

"OK, but you, you were the good bit. You saved us. Thank you. You saved our lives. I like the good people here and I like people. Some people very much..." she added, smiling shyly.

Matt laughed, feeling a bit sheepish. He wasn't sure quite how to respond to the last part. But he did feel proud and happy that he had helped to work things out. He couldn't explain how it had made him feel worthwhile again. That in a strange way she had probably saved him too. He realised that Murdo probably couldn't make promises, but he decided to talk to him about the strength of the guarantee and if that didn't work, he would enlist Kate's help to launch a campaign or something and if all else failed, he could always marry her. That thought brought him up short. She was leaning on his chest. He squeezed her against him. He didn't find the thought of marriage odd but the fact that it didn't worry him was definitely strange. A lot had changed in his life over the last couple of weeks but now wasn't the time to discuss such things; they needed to ensure that Parson and his gang went away for a very long time. Then they could address the future... and maybe be friends. That settled, Marieke was keen to know all about Iona's baby. Matt showed her photos and updated her on baby Ben's progress.

They were interrupted by the policewoman offering to order a takeaway for dinner. They chose their food from a takeaway menu, eating on the couch, not wanting to be more than a couple of feet apart at any time.

As the evening wore on, they bathed Kazik and settled him to bed. Marieke asked how long he could stay for. He didn't know. She also asked if he would come back. He didn't know that either. He told her that he would want to but they might not like it, because it could be seen as a security risk if one of Parson's friends was watching and tried to follow him. She seemed to understand, but looked disappointed. He held both her hands and reassured her... "After the trial, there will be lots of time ... if you want?"

"Yes," she nodded. "I want." Her eyes filled with tears as she held onto his hands tightly. She typed into the phone. "I scared without you...what if they come here? Why can't I stay with you?"

"The Police will keep you safe now. It will be better for the trial for us to be separate. I will keep in contact through Murdo with you."

They sat closely together on the sofa talking about some of the moments during their week. How they felt about them, both good and bad. They even managed to laugh at some aspects. They eventually ended up holding each other as the sun set behind the blind. Every now and again they could hear the policewoman clattering around in the kitchen, or up and down the stairs. After darkness fell outside, there was a knock on the living room door. Not waiting for a response, the protection officer leaned around the door.

"Your car will be here in twenty minutes to take you back." Matt's heart sank. He started to translate but Marieke knew already.

"You go now," she whispered, her eyes moist again.

He didn't trust himself to reply. He knew that leaving her there was the safest way and his only real option but it hurt in a way he had not experienced before to walk away and leave both mother and child, especially as he knew it might be a while before they saw each other again.

She followed him out into the hall, and held his hand while he placed the hood over his head. He could hear her quietly sobbing behind the closed door as he was led out to the car. Sitting in the back of the car he was glad of the hood to hide his emotions from the driver.

It was after midnight by the time he reached his hotel room. He kicked off his shoes and sat on the bed. Switched the TV on for the noise but didn't really watch it. He fell asleep on the bed, still dressed and with the bedside light on. He was emotionally drained, but intended to have his wits about him for the meeting with Murdo in the morning.

Waking early, Matt decided to go for a run around the Hotel complex to clear his mind. An energetic run was how he'd used to start his day, it cleared his head and sharpened his senses. It seemed apt to start again now.

By the time he returned, showered and indulged in the hotel's full Scottish breakfast, Murdo was waiting for him as he sauntered into the lounge.

"Enjoy your visit?"

"Yes thanks," replied Matt as he sat down. He wasn't going to go into details about any aspect of their discussions until he had heard what Murdo had to say. He sat back in the spacious hotel couch and smiled, obviously waiting for Murdo to begin.

"Well laddie, it's been quite a time, hasn't it? Firstly, I have to say thank you. We couldnae have done it without you. Green has gained consciousness and is singing like a canary. Evans is claiming that Parson blackmailed him into being involved over some indiscretion in the back of a cop car in the valleys. So, the slime ball is on his own, we're going to get him."

"Who's we?" Interjected Matt.

"Ah, well let me start at the beginning. I'm a consultant. I work for the Scottish Office. Now's not the time to discuss how I got the job but the powers that be felt the need to have a trustworthy person who would kick over the stones that the Poileas were scared to pick up and investigate the smells that others would rather avoid." He shrugged. "It keeps me busy and takes out a few of the bad guys who are in places they really shouldnae be." Matt was listening intently. He noticed how Murdo had slipped into the vernacular, not sounding quite as "posh." Was that because he was being more honest, he wondered, or was it all part of the act? But he wanted to hear more and Murdo continued, "I solve problems that others find too difficult, either because they are too close to home or just need that extra push that the Poileas would not want to give. Of course, I have to work within the law but every now and then the law needs a wee hand, as you just found out... A couple of years ago, the Met became aware not just of the high number of deaths of prostitutes in South London, but the appalling clearance rate of the local force and wanted me to look at their apparent inability to investigate these deaths. I started digging. I knew that officers were implicated, but I was looking to see how high the involvement went, when Marieke made her bolt for freedom. I was following Green and Evans as they were following her. I have now tracked down the pathologist who interrupted them at the house. They had beaten her up and left her for dead under the Westway. She is in hospital recovering, slowly unfortunately but is getting there. The news that they had been arrested has given her a real boost, there were those who were trying to claim she was hysterical or hallucinating by saying she had been attacked by policemen. I'm looking into them as well as that Inspector Bird who came to help us with our investigations. The DNA in the samples that were retrieved by your sister has implicated Parson, so we have him banged to rights for the murder in London. Marieke's and your own testimony prove his actions afterwards and confirm him as the leader of the gang. A job well done. Thank you." He reached into his jacket pocket and pulled out a slim brown envelope and placed it on the table. Pushing it towards Matt he continued, "This is not for your testimony ... your involvement with the Poileas here on in, is as a responsible citizen. But I've been paid for taking Parson and co. out of circulation and that couldn't have been done without your help, so I thought it only right that I cover your time and expenses." Matt looked at the envelope but didn't take it from the table. "What about Marieke? What about her time and expenses?"

"That's a bit more complicated. She is an illegal immigrant. But here she is viewed as the victim of trafficking rather than as a prostitute. We are giving her the appropriate support for that. Interpol are investigating the trafficking gang all the way back to Romania. I have argued that Marieke could be endangered if she returns there unprotected and that we have a duty of care especially as UK Police Officers were involved in putting her in that predicament. I think I am being listened to. She wants to go back to college; she's a clever resourceful girl."

"Aye, I know." Satisfied, Matt picked up the envelope and put it in his pocket. It was reasonably heavy; obviously filled with notes. He would see how much when he was alone.

Murdo smiled and continued. "Let's get this case closed off and those three mugs in jail. Then moving forward…" he seemed to become conspiratorial again, looking around him, pulling his chair in and leaning forward... "here's the thing, since the formation of Police Scotland, my workload has definitely increased. And as you may have noticed, I don't like to admit it, but I am not as young and fit as I used to be. I maybe, have other wee jobs that you could help me with."

Matt could feel the weight of the envelope in his pocket and remembered the sense of satisfaction he had at seeing Marieke and Kazik safe and well. Could this be a way to earn a living? It would be worth considering. But could he trust Murdo?

"We would always have to be the good guys," he looked Murdo straight in the eye. The Glaswegian didn't flinch. "And the pay would have to be worthwhile."

The Glaswegian smiled. "I'm sure I can more than reassure you on both counts. We're the good guys all right. It's just that every now and then we lend a hand, when the law might need a wee shove in the right direction."

Matt felt content. It seemed that in one day he had found a potential girlfriend and a possible job. The sun was shining and life was looking up, he had found a purpose again. Sorting Parson and his crew had been more rewarding than he had thought and he hadn't even counted the money in his pocket yet. He felt useful again and that was, he realised, all he had actually wanted. It wasn't about being a Marine... it was about being himself. He finished his coffee. Placing the cup on the table, he leant forward.

"One more thing I'd like to know..." Murdo waited... "What were you doing on Ben Mhor last Christmas?" Murdo sat back and sighed. "That, laddie, is another story."

###

About the Author

Brought up in North London, Libby Patterson studied Politics and Sociology gaining her Degree from Sunderland University. She moved to the Western Isles in 2006 through a work transfer opportunity. She has three grown up children, a son and twin daughters; She now lives in South Uist with her greyhounds and partner.

In 2012 Libby was made redundant and decided it was time to fulfil a lifelong ambition to write a novel. She attended a Crime Writer's Workshop with Caro Ramsay, and that is where Matt MacAulay came to life.

Libby cares passionately about the strength of the community and family values and believes the people of Uist have much to teach the people of wider Scotland and beyond.

36356486R00086

Printed in Great Britain
by Amazon